Dragonflies are not mythical creatures.

They are powerful and agile flyers noted for both strength and beauty.

Able to fly farther and higher than other winged insects, they have the capability of migrating across the sea.

Rise Up & Fly

A story of betrayal

B.J. Flemmings

Thank you to the people
who taught me these lessons,

For now I am stronger.
I let you go and the hurt dissolves.

Published By

Vabella Publishing

PO Box 1052

Carrollton, Georgia 30112

COPYRIGHT © 2022 B. J. FLEMMINGS

ISBN: 978-1-957479-43-9

PRINTED IN THE UNITED STATES OF AMERICA

Dedication

I would like to dedicate this book to all the ladies out there that have gained the courage to find their worth in the beauty of their being.

May your self confidence and gratitude be your armor against those that would attempt to lessen your purity of soul, and the innate beauty our Lord has bestowed upon us.

Acknowledgements

I would love to acknowledge my fierce friends who said I could, when I thought I couldn't.

A big thank you to you all. You know who you are.

Dragonflies can rotate each of their wings independently, giving them the ability to fly backwards, up, and down.

1

*V*anessa looked into the mirror to assess the job she'd done dressing for her first date with Daryl. Blue dress, not too short, low heels, good for walking, but still sexy. "Yep, hair and makeup look good." She smiled to her reflection. "I'm ready."

She'd been flirting with Daryl for three months online. He was a handsome man by his pictures. Her heart fluttered with the anticipation of meeting him in person.

At exactly 6:00 p.m., a dark blue mustang pulled into the driveway. Vanessa quickly put Bella in her crate. "OMG! I'm so nervous." She almost tripped when she heard the doorbell.

Vanessa opened the door, and there stood this tall handsome man, with a neatly trimmed goatee. His attire showed his muscular physique. Tight fitting casual t-shirt with nice dress slacks that complimented him very well.

"Daryl?"

He put his finger up to his forehead and with an air of confidence said, "The one and only."

"It's great to finally meet you in person instead of online," said Vanessa.

"I know, right?" Daryl said with a smile.

"Well." Vanessa looked at her watch. "Shall we go?"

Daryl nodded, smiled, and taking her by the arm, led her to the Mustang.

It was the longest ride Vanessa had ever taken. She felt happy, scared, nervous, and excited, all bottled together.

"So, Vanessa, is it dinner and a movie? Or just dinner."

"I think just dinner would be fine, I have work tomorrow."

Daryl pulled up to the porte-cochere at Park 75. She'd heard of it, but never thought in a million years she would be eating at such an upscale restaurant.

A young man went to Daryl's side and opened the door. Vanessa sat in amazement. *I'm so glad I dressed nice.* Daryl came to her door, opened it, and gently clasped her hand to help her out of the car.

Once they entered the restaurant, a waiter took them to a candlelit table covered with linen. Vanessa felt dizzy with excitement when Daryl pushed in her chair. *'Some Enchanted Evening'* played softly in the background.

Vanessa looked at the entrées on the menu. *The prices!* She fidgeted with the napkin. "I really don't know what I want."

"Maybe I can help. I've never had the salmon with wild rice, but I hear it's amazing. I usually order the steak."

"Salmon is one of my favorite seafoods."

Daryl motioned for the waiter. "The lady will have the salmon with wild rice, and I'll have the steak, medium well." He took the menu, closed it, and handed it to the waiter. He turned to Vanessa. "What wine would you like with dinner?"

"Vanessa looked into Daryl's deep brown eyes. They sparkled in the candlelight. "I prefer a light red."

"Great. I know just the one." He caught the sommelier's attention and lifted his chin.

The wine steward walked over, a white linen cloth over his arm. "Ready to order, sir?"

"Yes, we'd like a bottle of Pinot Noir?" Daryl said. He turned his attention to Vanessa and smiled.

"You seem very familiar with this restaurant. You must have dinner here a lot." Vanessa commented.

"Yes, I eat here frequently. I enjoy treating myself. I know it's pricey, but being an engineer, that really doesn't matter." Daryl raised his right eyebrow, and smiled smugly.

Vanessa wasn't sure what to think about that smile. However, more intrigued than weary, she said, "So, *I'm* being treated tonight, *too*. It's certainly a special night." She fell silent as the waiter brought the wine and poured for Daryl to taste.

Daryl nodded his approval and their glasses were filled.

Vanessa sipped her wine. "I do remember you mentioning you were an engineer on your profile."

"Oh, yes. I'm quite a successful one, to be honest. I should be traveling overseas soon, but I hope not too soon. I need to know you much better before I'll have the heart to leave you." Daryl dramatically put his hand to his heart.

Vanessa gave a tentative smile, flattered, but confused. She mulled over Daryl's flattering comment about going overseas and the incredible experience of such a fine restaurant and wondered. *Can he mean what he just said? We don't even know each other, but he seems so sincere.*

Another waiter approached with a huge tray on his shoulder, carrying their dinner. He served Vanessa, then Daryl.

"Thank you, Frank. It smells as delicious as ever." Daryl breathed deeply, smiled then exhaled.

"I hope you'll enjoy it, Mr. Nuygen. It's a pleasure to see you again." Frank smiled and looked at Vanessa. "And in such lovely company."

Frank bowed slightly and left them to their meal.

Deciding to ponder, rather than respond to his flattery, she picked up the silver fork, and pulled loose a piece of salmon, releasing the aroma of sea and herbs. Her mouth watered. She closed her eyes, savoring the taste. "Mm. This is so good."

"I agree with you there. My knife goes through this steak like it's butter. It literally melts in my mouth." He dabbed his napkin to the side of his mouth.

"I may be moving too fast for you, but I feel in my soul I've known you forever. I want to take our relationship to the next level—"

Vanessa's eyes grew huge. He immediately attempted to mend her shock.

"No, no, you may not understand." He held his hand out defensively and smiled. "I'm a very determined man. Physically, I'll take things as slow as you want. But, Vanessa, when I see what's right for me, I know it."

He reached out and clasped her hand. "And you are right for me. These last three months, you are the only person of substance I've communicated with. You're witty, you're fun, you're a professional woman that takes things seriously."

"But, Daryl, I—"

"Wait, my love." He raised her hand to his lips and kissed it. "I'm just asking for a chance. A chance to show you I'm worthy of your attention, and in time, perhaps, your affection." He sighed deeply. "I guess what I'm asking is if you'll cancel your Elite Singles account, and any other accounts of that type. I don't want you distracted by other men. Most of them are not true, and I don't want you to be taken in; not when I'm here to protect you."

Vanessa sat in stunned silence. Her cheeks burned and her heart raced. She watched as he sat, seemingly waiting patiently for an answer.

"Of course, I'll do the same. I have no need to speak to any woman but you. I feel as though our souls are connected." He lowered his eyes and withdrew his hands. "Of course, I've probably just made a fool of myself. I may have misread you. You may not even want a secure, or permanent relationship." He picked up his fork and knife. "I apologize for my presumptions."

"Oh, no, it's not that." Vanessa's heart was in a panic. Was she throwing away a chance of attaining what she'd dreamt of for years? "It's just so fast. But I feel a connection to you, too, Daryl. I do want a permanent relationship." She sighed.

"It's all I've ever wanted. It's just that I'm frightened. I'm frightened of making a mistake, and I'm frightened I might lose my chance at happiness." Vanessa picked up her wine glass and sipped. *I too, feel our souls have touched. Is this a dream?*

"If all you're asking is that I delete my account, I don't have a problem with that. Let's just give us a little more time. Is that all right?" Her heart fluttered in trepidation—waiting to soar on the wings of hope.

"My lady." He bowed his head, sliced off a piece of steak and held it in the air. "It will be my pleasure proving to you I'm worthy. I love romance, and I'm simply in love with the idea of wooing you, my heart's desire." He smiled, put his bite in his mouth, and closed his eyes in reverence of the moment, as well as the taste of steak.

After dinner on the way home, an inkling of doubt crossed Vanessa's mind, just a fleeting whisper. *No, I won't be a dunce and ruin this for myself. I must stop being so insecure. I am just as beautiful as he is handsome. And I am a successful woman. I may not make as much money as he does, but I can take care of myself.*

He helped her from the car and walked her to the house. "Don't forget to lock the door."

"I deserve this." She'd closed the door behind her after Daryl's kiss turned to passion and he'd driven away, leaving her wanting.

The dragonfly symbolizes change,
transformation, adaptability,
and self-realization.

2

*O*n cloud nine the next day, Vanessa hummed while applying her makeup, which she never wore to work. Then, before walking out the door, she went to her computer to delete her Elite Singles account. *Am I doing the right thing?* Her finger hovered over the button. She took a deep breath, a huge smile came across her face. She pushed the button. "That's it. I'm trusting you, Daryl." She kissed her puppy goodbye and headed to work.

"Well, look at Miss Hollywood with her face on today," exclaimed John in records. "What's the occasion?"

Vanessa flapped her hand at her tall thin co-worker. "You just mind your own business, John Hawkins, and keep your nose out of everybody else's, especially mine," Vanessa said with her huge smile still in place.

"Oh, dear. I smell romance in the air." He turned back to his computer and clucked his tongue.

"Hi, Susan. Are you still here?" Vanessa waved to the night shift tech.

"Yeah, I had to work over. One of our patients had a rough night, so I just stuck with him." Normally Susan answered questions with one or two words, if she answered at all. This was quite a proclamation.

"It wasn't Mr. Smith, was it? I've been a little concerned he might backslide," said Vanessa.

"No, no. It was Mr. Watkins, in room 208, and he's much stronger this morning." She gave Vanessa a brief smile. "Say, you look great this morning."

"Personally, I think both of you got some last night. Vanessa's wearing makeup, and you, Susan, have said more in the last few minutes than I've heard from you in the year I've known you," John piped in. "Do tell, do tell."

They all chuckled.

Susan made a shooing motion at him. "Never kiss and tell, John; never kiss and tell."

Vanessa's cheeks burned. *Mine's just wishful thinking. Maybe soon, though.* She said, "I don't know about you two, but I've got work to do." She turned and went to her ward with a bounce in her step.

She got her respirator from the station and went to her first patient. She peered around the door to Mr. Smith's room.

"Hold on to your socks, I'm coming in fully loaded, Mr. Smith." She pushed her cart into his room.

"I heard you and that squeaky wheel of yours all the way down the hall. I had time to dress, shave, have breakfast, and get myself into this chair." Mr. Smith's chuckle turned into a coughing fit.

"No sneaking up on you, you're too sly." Vanessa reached down and hugged the old man. "I won't mention that I spoke with nurse Janice this morning." She winked at him and began to mix his solution according to his chart.

"Okay, ya caught me in a fib. Nurse Janice helped me with all that an hour ago." He beamed up at her. "You look positively smashing this morning, my dear. I see a sparkle in your eyes that can only mean there's a special gentleman involved."

"There's no fooling a wise old fox like you, Mr. Smith. I did have a date last night. And he turned out to be a *very* special gentleman, indeed," said Vanessa. "It's hard to find those nowadays."

"You're a very fortunate young lady. I'm happy for you. I hope everything works out well. Now, get on with your torture for the day, then you can tell them to let me out of this jail and send me home," he coughed once more.

"Mr. Smith, you're too funny for your own good. I think I'll tell the doctor you need to stay another two weeks." She went to place the breathing apparatus over his nose and mouth for his treatment.

His hand shot up and grabbed her arm gently. "Oh, no. If you do that, I'll find that young man of yours and tell him how mean you are to me, and you'll be the same to him. He just might come and spring me out of this jail."

Vanessa said her goodbye with a kiss on Mr. Smith's cheek. She had a great affinity for the old gentleman. He suffered from pulmonary distress as a result of contracting pneumonia while in the hospital. No one knew when he'd be able to go home, if ever.

The memory of Daryl's kiss flooded her thoughts and replaced any sadness she had with a feeling of thrilling happiness.

She headed down to her department to clean her machine and refill her solutions for the next patient.

The day shift supervisor was just inside the door. "Hi, Sheila. How are you this morning?" Vanessa had always liked Sheila. They'd worked together for a couple of years. She was strict, but fair. Though she'd always distanced herself from most of the staff. Vanessa supposed she'd had to, being a supervisor.

"I'm good. Say, you look great, today. Not that you don't always look good, you just seem to have a special glow this morning."

"Thank you. I'm in a very good mood today," Vanessa nodded with a smile.

Sheila took her by the arm and pulled her into an alcove where the computers were kept.

"Listen, Vanessa. You're a great tech, and I don't want to see you get in trouble," she said softly. "I was looking over Friday's level entries and it appeared that you had given a patient the incorrect formula—"

Vanessa gasped and put her hand over her mouth.

"Wait, wait. You didn't—even if you had, there would not have been serious adverse effects—but you didn't. You simply made the wrong entries in the computer. I checked their charts and they were marked correctly."

Vanessa took a deep shaky breath, her face hot with shame and embarrassment.

Sheila continued, "So, I made the necessary corrections in the computer and finalized them."

Vanessa's eyes brimmed, her shaking body betrayed the state of her nerves.

Sheila reached out and hugged her. "Hey, everybody has missteps. I've had my share, for sure. I know you're excellent at what you do—you're the best we've got. I just wanted you to know, so you can be extra careful."

Sheila hugged her again. "Hey, how about we go out for a drink after work? You up for that?"

Vanessa wiped her eyes and smiled feebly. She took a hitching breath, and said, "I'd like that, Sheila, thanks."

The rest of the day, Vanessa chastised herself for being so careless. She'd been so excited about meeting Daryl for their first date, she'd been distracted. She'd made a clumsy mistake. *Well, I won't do that again. This is my livelihood—these are my patients, and nothing is worth jeopardizing either one.*

She got her coat, purse, and keys, and headed to her car to meet Sheila. *Oh, God, I hope he calls tonight.*

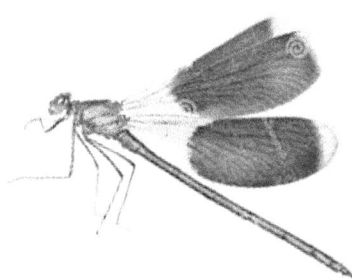

The change dragonflies symbolize refers to mental and emotional maturity, and understanding the deeper meaning of life.

3

Vanessa walked into Sparks and looked around for Sheila. She was excited about the possibility of having a friend, but was a little nervous that Sheila might not like her.

I don't know how relaxed I can be. She's my boss, after all. But Sheila had been so nice to her today when she'd told Vanessa about her mistake. *Well, it won't hurt to just stay on my guard.*

She spotted Sheila sitting at the bar, waved, and worked her way through the crowded restaurant.

"Hey." Vanessa smiled nervously.

"Hey, yourself." Sheila lifted her handbag off the seat next to her. "I saved you a seat."

"Thanks." Vanessa sat down. "What are you drinking? It looks refreshing."

"Gin and tonic, and it is. Would you like one?"

"That sounds nice." Vanessa signaled for the bartender.

They sat chatting lightly about their private lives. Sheila was married with three kids. The youngest was in sixth grade, the oldest a sophomore in high school. She loved her family, but she found her life a bit boring.

Vanessa talked about the son she'd raised on her own, and what a joy her grandchildren were. She was hesitant to go into her deeper feelings of loneliness, and a little embarrassed to tell of her excitement at falling for someone she met online. *I think I'll play my cards a little closer to the vest for now.*

As she was talking, she noticed Sheila glancing frequently over to the tables. Vanessa followed her gaze and saw a very tall, handsome man sitting at a table with a woman whose back was turned to the bar. She seemed completely unaware the man was looking over her shoulder at Sheila. *Is she flirting with him?*

Sheila must have noticed Vanessa had grown quiet. She turned her head back and blinked. "I'm sorry, I got distracted. Say, let's go relax at a table, I feel like we're on stage up here."

"Sure, good idea. I don't like these tall stools, anyway." Vanessa smiled.

They gathered their bags and drinks. Leading the way, Sheila went to a vacant two-top within direct line of sight to the handsome man she'd been flirting with.

After a few drinks, they decided to have tacos for dinner. They both got a little tipsy, but had a great time. Sheila flirted blatantly and at one point put her hand to the side of her mouth and stage whispered, "Check out that hunk," she pointed behind her hand. "No ring." She winked at Vanessa and giggled.

Vanessa felt as though her smile was frozen on her face. She almost said, *you've* got one, but didn't.

When they'd collectively decided to call it a night and go home, Vanessa said, "Won't your husband be worried about you?"

"Nah, it's good for him to wonder once in a while. It keeps the juices flowing if you know what I mean." She elbowed Vanessa in the ribs and walked to her car.

Vanessa was unsure of what to think of their evening together. The laughter was great, the girl-talk so much fun. Sheila was comfortable with herself and didn't care much of what others thought of her, a quality Vanessa had striven for, for so long. But she was quite sure that Sheila was heading for disaster in her marriage. She hoped it was look and not touch, but she wondered. And though their friendship was newly formed—she cared a great deal for Sheila's happiness and well-being.

*   *   *

The next week at work Vanessa got two new patients that spun her workload into a hectic pace.

She hadn't heard from Daryl, but she was too busy during her work day, and too exhausted at night to worry about it.

She walked into records at a brisk pace. "Thank God it's Friday," she said to John.

"Girl, you look like you're getting off shift after a long day instead of coming in," John said.

"It's been a rough week, John, but it's at an end and I couldn't be happier." Vanessa sighed and pulled the files she needed for the day.

Susan ran through the door, her face a mask of weariness and alarm. "Vanessa." She grabbed Vanessa's arm. "Mr. Smith started agonal breathing at 1:00 a.m., he went into cardiac arrest, but we got it under control about an hour ago—I know how close you are—"

"Is he conscious?" Vanessa was shaking. She looked down at the records in her hand, then at John, then Susan.

John got up from his computer. "Go on, I'll log your files out for you." He grabbed the files, noted down the names, shoved them back in her arms and shooed her out the door.

"Thanks, John," Susan said over her shoulder, running after Vanessa.

* * *

Vanessa drug herself into the house and collapsed on the couch. Bella jumped up into her lap and kissed her face. "Hi, sweetie, I'll get your dinner in a minute, just let me rest awhile."

Mr. Smith had gained consciousness just before the end of her shift. He was still in intensive care. They'd taken him off the breathing machine, but his pallor was deathly pale. She said a prayer for her elderly friend and got up to put something together for dinner.

She was lounging on her patio in the chair beside her mother's pink rose bush. Her after dinner wine had loosened her muscles, lessening her stress. She started to relax and gave her worry for Mr. Smith over to hopeful thoughts.

The phone rang. "Hey darlin', did ya miss me?" came Daryl's voice over the phone.

A thrill ran through her. "To tell you the truth I've been so busy I really didn't have time to." Vanessa was too tired to smile.

"Well, I've got news. I don't know how you're going to take it. But I swear to God, baby, it's not my fault. My company didn't give me a choice, I've been on the run since our dinner last week." He paused. It sounded like he was taking a drink, ice cubes rattled in a glass.

"Babe? Ya there?" he asked.

"I'm here, Daryl, I'm just tired. One of my patients—"

"Great, great. Now, like I was trying to tell you, I'm calling you from Belgium."

* * *

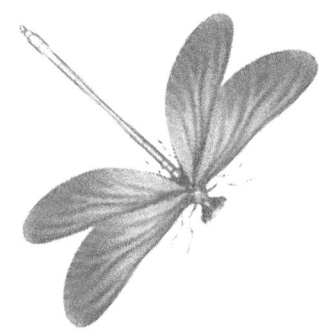

Among the most ancient creatures, dragonflies were some of the first winged insects to evolve over 300 million years ago.

4

*M*r. Smith had been out of intensive care for three days. Vanessa peeked her head around the door of his room. He was still pale and very weak, but he was on the mend.

"There's my little dragonfly lady. What are you doing sneaking around here?" Mr. Smith's voice was barely above a whisper.

"I figured I'd come and spy on you; make sure you're not planning the great escape." She walked over to his bed and gave him a hug. "I miss you. Since I can't give you your treatments for a while, I thought I'd fly over here real quick for my hug."

"You don't want to make that gentleman friend of yours jealous, do you?"

"Nah, don't you worry about him. He's all the way over in Belgium," she said.

Mr. Smith started coughing. "There, there, now." She fluffed his pillow and raised his bed slightly, freeing his air passage. "Better?"

He nodded.

"Don't say anything, Mr. Smith. I've worn you out enough. I'll come check on you before I go home." She leaned over and kissed his forehead.

After drinks with Sheila, Vanessa called it an early night. Daryl was supposed to call again tonight. A shiver of pleasure went through her at the thought of their call two nights ago.

The steamy passion of his husky voice had brought her to climax numerous times.

She made her dinner and fed Bella, then settled down in front of the television to await his call.

She waited.

And waited.

She drug herself to bed just after 1:00 a.m., telling herself he must have slept through the time he'd said he'd call. Considering the time difference, it made sense.

The days passed. Mr. Smith was recovering nicely; she'd be able to administer his breathing treatments again next week.

Each lonely night, her angst grew. *Maybe he found someone else. There's nothing that special about me.* She looked at Bella curled up beside her on the couch and stroked her black and brown silken hair.

"It's been forever, Bella. I guess we just need to give up. It was a pipe dream, anyway."

The phone rang.

She jumped for the phone on her end table.

"Hey, girl. I missed you for drinks tonight." Sheila's voice lilted over the phone.

"Oh, it's you." Vanessa's heart sank to her knees.

"Well, gosh. That's some greeting." Sheila sounded a little hurt.

"I'm sorry, Sheila. I thought it was my guy in Belgium."

"No sweat. I get ya. How long's it been this time?" she asked, concern in her voice for her friend.

"Going on two weeks. I just need to forget it. I don't know what he saw in me anyway," said Vanessa, her voice despondent.

"Oh, no. I'm not going to let you go down that road, sunshine. You're beautiful and worth a whole hell of a lot more than any man could possibly give you. If he isn't seriously delayed for a good reason, which is probably the case, then he's not worth spit, and you don't need a loser, girlfriend."

"I guess I'm just feeling sorry—"

The phone beeped with an incoming call.

Vanessa looked at her phone, saw Daryl's number and shouted, "It's him, gotta go." She clicked over.

Daryl explained away his absence by an over load of work. His voice held remorse as he told her how he'd missed her beautiful voice and longed to look into her eyes when he could finally make love to her for real.

Two hours later, she fell into a blissful sleep.

It was three weeks before Daryl called again. Vanessa was even lower than she'd been with his first lapses in communication. Instead of her previous exuberance at his calling, she was wary.

"Daryl, it's been three weeks. I really don't understand," she began.

"I know, sweetheart. I'm so sorry. I had an accident. I broke my ankle and bruised some ribs. I just got out of the hospital. They kept me for observation so long I thought I'd go mad." He sighed. "Forgive me?"

"Oh, my goodness, Daryl. What happened? I'm so sorry I was angry and hurt. I should have known something had happened."

"Oh, honey, I don't blame you. Don't feel bad. I was crossing the street and a car just barely grazed me. They're crazy drivers here. The doctors wanted to make sure I didn't have internal injuries—that's why they kept me so long."

"But you're all right? God, I miss you." Vanessa had tears in her eyes.

"I'm fine, baby. And I have good news and bad news. I'll just start with the good news. I'm over the top about it. You ready?" he asked.

"Oh, God, Daryl," she laughed. "Yes, tell me." Her excitement swelled.

"I'm coming home in the next four to six weeks, baby. Can you stand it? God, I can't wait to get my hands on you."

"Oh, how wonderful, Daryl. My heart's just pounding." Tears of happiness brimmed her eyes.

"The only drawback, and I know you'll help out, babe, I need some money to get me there. You have savings, don't you?"

Vanessa was taken aback, her breath caught in her throat. When she next spoke, her voice felt tiny.

"How much do you need?"

"I can get it back to you within a week, so don't worry about that. The hospital wouldn't let me go until I paid them every dime—it wiped me out." He fell silent.

Her heart was in her throat. She had to force the words out. "How much, Daryl?"

"I need $5,000, babe." He continued, "I know it's a lot of money, but I'll have it back to you in a week. I swear."

"Daryl, I don't have that kind of money." She clenched her hands. She was torn between feeling betrayed and wanting desperately to believe him.

"Not even in savings?" He sounded as though he didn't believe her.

Warning signals went off at the tone of his voice.

"Not even in savings, Daryl. I was a single mother for 20 years, I had college tuition, braces, illness—you name it." She hesitated, "And frankly, if I did have it, I'm not so sure I would lend it to you, anyway."

"Oh, babe, don't be that way. We mean too much to each other. Listen, just send me what you can, it'll help me get out of this country and into your beautiful arms. You can do a bank transfer." He waited.

She was silent.

"Babe?"

She was silent.

"Look, I'll get to you however I can. You mean too much to me. I'll be there for you. Then maybe we can talk about a more permanent relationship. I need you in my life."

Confusion overwhelmed her. "I'll see what I can do, Daryl." Her voice hitched. She just wanted to get off the phone and think. "I'll see what I can do, I've got to go now, good bye."

She hung up, her head swirling. She was off the next day. That would give her time to think things through.

5

Saturday morning found Vanessa lounging on her couch in her pajamas and bath-robe. Bella was lying beside her, accepting every piece of dry sugar-coated cereal her mistress offered.

After an hour of 'one for you, one for me,' Vanessa said, "Okay, girl. Let's get us some real breakfast, then, I'll decide what to do."

She went to the kitchen, scrambled some eggs for herself and treated Bella to a can of dog food.

I just don't know what to do. Is he telling me the truth? What if he really is stranded in another country?

Then another part of her mind kicked in and she imagined him just disappearing—with her money.

"Well, the least I can do is call the bank and see if I can even borrow that much," she told Bella.

She plopped back down on the couch, put her slipper-clad feet on the scarred coffee table, and dialed the bank.

After speaking to Mr. Milton, the loan officer she'd known from when she and her ex had purchased the house, she was a roller coaster of emotions. Mr. Milton had assured her that, yes, she could very easily attain a $5,000 signature loan.

She felt the pressure of indecision. Helping because she could, or withholding assistance because of mistrust, took turns weighing heavily from one side to the other like a seesaw.

She broke down and cried.

Bella came and licked her cheek. Vanessa hugged her little Yorkie, dried her tears, and sighed. "You're right Bella. I don't even know this man that well, and look at me." She blew her nose. "If I'm this torn up about not trusting him with my hard-earned money, what would a future with him be like? Going off to different countries, turning up needy.

She scratched Bella behind her ear. "What say we just leave it status quo. I don't need to entertain the idea of lending anyone that amount of money." Bella barked her agreement.

"Okay, let's see what they've got on TV today." Vanessa snuggled down with her puppy and flipped through the channels.

She gasped; her heart in her throat. Fumbling with the remote, she struggled to raise the volume, but dropped it twice. Finally, she could hear the host all too clearly. "You say there have been five women now, that claim to have given you money for one reason or another?"

Daryl nodded. "That's right, Ms. Hall. Actually, one woman contacted me. I reached out to the police and they discovered another four victims. The police informed me that a man, looking very much like myself, had stolen my identity and posted all my personal photos on a dating site, posing as an engineer. So far, he's taken a total of $70,000 from five women that they know of."

Vanessa sat with her mouth agape. The hammer blow to her chest took her breath away. "That's not Daryl. That's not Daryl."

She sat rigid, shaking her head back and forth with tears streaming down her face.

"Dr. Richardson, what steps have you had to take to get your life—indeed, your reputation back in order?" asked the host.

"It's not been easy. Thank heaven I published an article that contained my picture as the author, and that prompted the first lady to come forward, accusing me of taking $10,000 and disappearing on her. That's how I found out." The handsome Dr. shifted in his chair. "I was hoping the authorities could help this lady get her money back. But the emotional damage to these women is devastating."

The host took over. "So, everyone watching this program take heed. Guard your financial information, your home address, anything that is personally connected to you; especially when you're dealing with people online." The camera zoomed in on the host's face. "Ladies, if you've just met someone, in person or online, and you have the slightest suspicion they are not who they say they are, beware.

"If you have a photo, do a reverse image search—Social Catfish is the site for this. It's inexpensive and well worth the money."

The man she was falling in love with; the man she'd had phone sex with and desperately desired a more physical encounter; the man she'd been sitting here tearing herself apart about giving him $5,000; he wasn't even real. Nothing he'd said was real.

"I'm so ashamed. I'm such a fool!" At 11:00 a.m. on that Saturday morning, Vanessa got up and poured herself a drink. She sat down on the sofa with Bella in her arms to sob and drink the day away.

Monday morning found Vanessa with a roaring hangover. She got out of bed sick to her stomach with a splitting headache.

Oh, God. I'm not going to make it. She stumbled in the bathroom and vomited. After a bit of yogurt to settle her stomach, she called in sick to work.

Vanessa sat down on the couch, turned the TV on and shakily reached for the bottle on the floor beside her. *No. Stop this nonsense. You've got to get yourself together, girl. You're better than this.* "I'm tearing myself up over a dirt-bag."

She pulled herself up, took a shower, and got dressed. Very slowly her head cleared. She cleaned her house, made a list, and went grocery shopping. Tending to her usual weekend chores brought back a sense of normalcy.

She was at work, not necessarily bright, but at least early on Tuesday.

Everyone met her with a quiet smile, most making a point of not mentioning her haggard appearance. The exception was Mr. Smith.

"Ahh. My sunshine comes, but she is not shining," he said from his wheelchair.

Vanessa gave him a weak smile and pecked him on the forehead.

He patted her hand affectionately. "It will be all right, my dear. I will have my little dragonfly with her caramel-colored skin back in no time."

After work Sheila caught up with her. "Hey, you look dreadful. How about a girls' night out? You up for drinks at Sparks?"

"No, thanks, Sheila. I'm really not up to it." Vanessa didn't attempt to smile for her friend. "I'll see you tomorrow."

Vanessa slogged through the next few weeks. She likened it to pushing a string uphill, but she made it. Each day her smile came easier. She actually laughed a few times.

One Friday evening at home, Vanessa trusted herself enough to have a drink. Not worrying that she wouldn't be able to stop, as was the case of her lost weekend. The weekend she discovered the humility of betrayal.

She picked up the phone and dialed Sheila. "Hey."

"Hey, yourself. How are you? I've been worried." Sheila's cheerful voice came over the phone.

"I'm fine. Getting better all the time, thanks." Vanessa hesitated. "I missed our drinks together. I wanted to ask if you'd like to come to dinner at my house tomorrow night. You know, just us; no crowd, no looky loos, nobody's noise but ours.

What do you say?" Vanessa held her breath. A bit of that old fear of rejection poking its head up.

"I say, what time? That sounds fantastic."

"It's a date, then. See you at 7:00." Vanessa hung up, breathed deeply, and smiled to herself for the first time in almost a month.

6

V anessa walked out her back door onto her patio. After dinner and a shower, she wanted the peace and solitude of her tiny rose garden.

The sheer sleeve of her silken robe, which barely concealed her youthful shape, caught on a thorn. Her smile widened. "Hello, beauty." She disengaged herself, leaned down and smelled her mother's pink rose bush.

Vanessa sat down in the lounge chair between two Mr. Lincoln bushes. Their deep red blooms, as big as her hand, looked like velvet. From this spot she could sit and gaze at the magnificent pink flowers of her favorite bush. The stress and heartbreak of the past two months washed away. She felt empowered.

She sat and sipped her wine amidst her safe haven, breathing in the mix of incredible scents that always lifted her spirits. The sky over the neighbors' trees turned to a deep rose gold. *Time to get off to bed.* It was going to be a busy day tomorrow with Sheila coming for dinner.

Vanessa decided on tacos for dinner. She knew Sheila had liked them when they ate at Sparks. These would be even better, cooking them at home, adding her own flair. She decided on premium beef, freshly ground. She gestured to the butcher behind the glass to come out.

He smiled at her with a twinkle in his eyes. Their amber color was accented by his dark chocolate skin. "Morning, Ma'am. Can I help you?"

Vanessa felt heat rise in her cheeks and hoped she wasn't blushing. "I'd like a pound of freshly ground sirloin, please."

He raised his thin, arched eyebrows. "Mm mmm. Great choice. Special dinner?" His smile exposed brilliant white teeth.

She didn't know what to say. She wanted to blurt out—just a friend—or, no, just a girlfriend. Her mind raced in circles. *What is the matter with me?* "Umm, well, tacos." Her voice felt timid and small.

He chuckled. "Sounds good." He turned and went through the door to grind her beef.

When he came out and handed her the package, he said, "My name's Robert. Whenever you need anything, I'll be here. Have a good day."

"Thank you." Vanessa smiled, eyes sparkling. *I guess I'm not so bad, after all.* She went home in high spirits, feeling rather pretty.

The setting sun kissed the lace curtains on her kitchen window. The golden rays illuminated a tear at the bottom. *Oh, goodness, that's an eyesore. I need to repair that.* "Or better yet, I'll buy some new ones," she mused aloud.

*   *   *

Cheese and lettuce shredded, onions chopped, tomatoes diced, now for this beef. The aroma of spiced meat sauce made her mouth water. She lifted a spoonful to taste straight from the frying pan.

The doorbell rang.

"Thank goodness, I would have burned my mouth for sure." She put the spoon in the cradle and went to answer the door.

"Hey. Good to see you. Welcome to my humble abode." Vanessa opened the door wide and stepped back to let Sheila in.

Sheila held up a bottle, grinning widely. "I brought the wine."

Vanessa clapped her hand to her forehead. "Oh, my gosh. I completely forgot about wine." She shook her head and laughed. "That would never have done."

"You're forgiven. I've been dying for tacos all week, and if that's not what I smell, I'll drink one whole bottle myself."

"Well, bring that bottle in the kitchen before our dinner burns." Vanessa turned, got her favorite long stemmed glasses from the sideboard, and led Sheila to the kitchen.

"Oh, my God, these are delicious." Sheila pulled at the elastic band of her slacks. "That's why I wore these. Do you want that last one?"

Vanessa laughed and shook her head. "I'll pour us more wine. Then, when you're finished, we can go out to my little piece of heaven."

Sheila wiped her mouth on a napkin. "Sounds great. Grab that other bottle. I'll bring the glasses."

Halfway through the second bottle, both women were relaxed enough to let the conversation veer to more personal matters.

"So, you know I'm married with three kids. What about you?" Sheila asked.

"Well, my ex messed around on me when Gregory was two. So, that was the end of that. Neither one of us have seen him since. I did alright for myself. He finished school, and I have three beautiful grandkids who adore me." Vanessa sighed. "I do get lonely, though."

"Lonely? You? I can't believe you don't have a man in your life, girl. You're beautiful. That curly hair; those huge brown eyes. You light up everybody's life that talks to you. What's the problem?"

"Well, I just can't find anyone. I've tried some dating sites, but that really didn't turn out so well." The wound was still too raw for her to go into the episode with Daryl. It was too embarrassing. "I ended up feeling like a sucker. It seems everybody's just out to get what they want and to hell with you."

"It's tough out there," Sheila said, nodding.

"Maybe I'm old fashioned, but I want a partner. Someone that's comfortable sitting at the head of the table, if you know what I mean," Vanessa confided.

"Oh, I know what you mean, all right. I've got a man at the head of the table." She shook her head. "It's not all it's cracked up to be." She sipped her wine. "It's boring. I like a little strange every once in a while."

"Sheila!" Vanessa sat up straighter in her seat. "Your family, your kids."

"Oh, they're fine. Nobody knows anything. Steven doesn't pay attention to what I do. When I get home late, he's already asleep. The next day, he's a little spiced up. So, so much for the better."

"But, Sheila—"

"Oh, don't, 'but Sheila' me," she laughed. "It's fun. In fact, I've got one on the line right now.

You remember that guy at the restaurant?" Sheila raised her eyebrows up and down.

"But, you're married," Vanessa protested.

"Come to find out, so is he," Sheila grinned. "Lighten up, girl. Who cares if they're out for what they can get? You should be, too." Sheila drained her glass and got up. "I gotta run, Nessa. The sun set two hours ago. Walk me to the door?"

"Sure." Vanessa got up with her and led her through the house.

When they reached the door, Sheila turned and said, "I love your little slice of heaven, and your tacos are delicious. We should do this more often."

Thoughts raced through Vanessa's mind. Even though she didn't agree with Sheila's immoral treatment of her marriage, who was she to judge? Sheila was honest, and it was great to have someone to talk to. Vanessa wanted a friend.

"How about every Thursday night; here? We'll take turns cooking," Vanessa smiled.

"You read my mind. Thursdays are perfect," Sheila laughed and hugged her.

Vanessa watched her new friend drive away with hope in her heart for a brighter tomorrow.

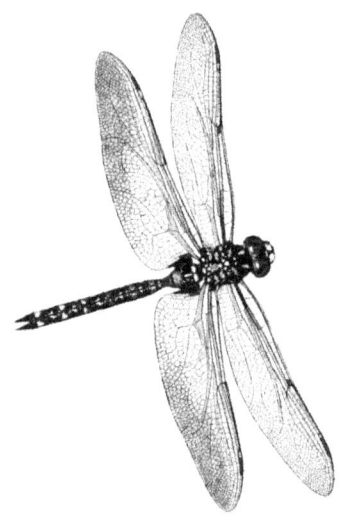

Dragonflies spend five to seven years underwater to accumulate enough mercury in their bodies, before the nymphs hatch.

7

*D*riving home from work, Vanessa passed the home outlet store. She'd had Sheila over for dinner three times now, and each time her kitchen curtains had caught her eye; that glaring hole still existed.

I need to do something about that. Why not right now?

She made a U-turn at the light and drove back toward the store. On the way, she glanced over and saw the gym. Until a few months ago, she'd gone there once or twice each week. *That's something else I need to do for myself.* She nodded once. *Maybe tomorrow.*

Vanessa straightened the curtains she'd just hung on her kitchen window. They were creamy yellow with delicate pink rose buds. *I brought a bit of you inside, Mama.* "Beautiful." She glanced around her; saw the uneven kitchen table, the rusted hinges on the corner cupboard, the old marked up counter top, and sighed. "Well, it's a start."

That evening after dinner, Vanessa sat on her threadbare couch holding Bella. Paying no attention to the television's talking heads, her mind wandered to the supermarket butcher. *What was his name?* She pondered. *Roger? No, Robert. That's it.*

She was thinking how nice it would be, sitting here with him after dinner instead of alone. *How would I bring that about? Do I even have the courage to ask him over?*

Her eyes wandered to the carpet in front of the hall bathroom. It was stained and torn. You could even see a dip where the floorboards were failing. "Who am I kidding? I can't bring anyone into my home in this state. Bella," she hugged her Yorkie close and kissed the top of her head," "We've got some work to do."

Vowing to take things slow, but get things done, she went to bed promising she'd work on her home as well as herself. She got out her gym clothes for after work the next day.

*   *   *

"Drinks after work?" Sheila shouted.

Vanessa waved at her from across the lot. "Not today, I'm headed to the gym."

"Woohoo. You go girl." She got in her car.

Vanessa had no doubt where Sheila was headed, Sparks. Over the weeks the two women had become close; Vanessa sharing her insecurities and hopes; Sheila telling of her affairs, past and current, interlaced with her husband's trusting ineptitude, and the antics of her children.

Sheila's current affair was with the Sparks patron Vanessa had noticed the first time they'd gone out for drinks. She'd been told all about it in much more detail than she was comfortable with.

But Sheila was supportive, and Vanessa appreciated a close friend; someone she could confide in, lean on, and have a great many laughs with.

She walked out of the dressing room and headed for the treadmill. She felt eyes on her and her cheeks felt flushed. But she was determined her shyness was not going to get the best of her. *You've got this. Keep going.* Looking down at the floor in front of her, she stepped up on the treadmill and began to walk.

Feeling silly she lifted her head and stared straight forward out the window. A deep voice came from right beside her.

"Hi, how are you?" Medium height, caramel colored skin like hers, he had a rugged, but kind face, and she liked it.

"I'm fine, thank you," she blushed.

"I'll say." He winked. "I'm Jim."

She continued walking, looking straight ahead, then turned and said, "Hi, Jim."

I'm not ready to plunge into anything. I plunged last time and look what happened.

As though he'd read her mind, he smiled and said, "I got it. I know you have a name, and maybe one day you'll let me know what it is. Sometimes I forget myself and move too fast." He bowed slightly at the waist. "Don't worry. You're safe with me, shy lady. I just wanted to tell you, you're beautiful." He quickened his pace and turned back to his exercise.

"Thank you," she said. And she meant it. She felt beautiful. With her big dark brown eyes sparkling, she smiled through the rest of her routine. She made a mental note of the day and time, thinking perhaps that's when she'd return.

Feeling uplifted with a permanent smile on her face, Vanessa decided to swing by the supermarket and see what meats were on special.

Not admitting to herself why she'd really come here, she sauntered up to the meat case and perused the different cuts. She wanted to look through the window in the back to see if she could spot Robert, but didn't want to seem forward. *Right, Vanessa. Just pick something up and leave before you make a fool of yourself.*

She grabbed a pack of chicken breasts and turned to go. "May I help you, Ma'am?"

"Uh, no thanks. I got it," she said, holding up her package. She quickly glanced over the young man's shoulder, saw no one else, smiled, and left.

On her way to the car she noticed someone waving to her a few cars down from hers. *I know him. Is that Lamar?*

She raised her hand and waved in return. She hadn't seen Lamar for years. In fact, she'd seen him and his wife in church one Easter Sunday. *I didn't know they still lived in the area. It's a small world.*

*   *   *

The phone rang as she put her key in the lock. She ran inside and picked it up.

"Hello?" She hadn't looked at caller ID.

"How was the gym?" Sheila's voice came over the phone.

"Oh, hi. I thought you were going for drinks," she said.

"I did. But he didn't show. Something must have come up with his wife. So I just went home and fed the kids." She laughed. "So, how was it? The gym."

"Interesting. I met a guy named Jim who told me I was beautiful. Can you believe it?"

"Of course, I believe it. So, when do you two get together?" Sheila asked conspiratorially.

"I don't know that we will. He doesn't even know my name," Vanessa confided.

"What?! What's wrong with you, Nessa? You could have 'Jim' there with you right now." Sheila chided.

"Not my style, girlfriend. I'm not sure I'm ready for anything. But I am working up to little flirtations here and there. So, be proud of me for getting that far."

"I guess so. Regardless, I'm proud of you anyway. You're making strides getting that scam artist out of your head."

"Yeah." She paused. "You know, I've been thinking seriously about giving my house a face lift. It needs so much work. Know of anyone I can hire?"

"No. Not off hand. It's a good idea, though. I love your new curtains."

"Thanks, me too. I think I'll call my cousin. He knows everybody and just about every thing there is to know. I'll keep you posted."

When she hung up, she immediately dialed her cousin Michael's, number. *He's gotta know a handyman; or at least steer me in the right direction. By hook or by crook, I'm going to make my home as beautiful as I am.*

Adult dragonflies have a life span as short as a week. If conditions are warm, and absent extreme weather, they can live as long as six months.

8

"You wouldn't believe the time I had last night." Sheila took a bite of her pizza and made a yummy sound.

Vanessa didn't know if it was from memory of her clandestine date or the cheese and pepperoni.

"That man. Oh, my God. You just wouldn't believe—"

"That's okay, I get the picture. No need for details, thanks." Vanessa took a bite and laughed around a mouthful.

"Oh, you're such a prude." Sheila flapped her hand at her friend. "So, what's new with you? Find anybody to fix you up?" Sheila burst out laughing. "Your house, I mean."

"Yes. At least I think so. I haven't called him yet." She set her wine glass on the table in her rose garden. "My cousin gave me his name and number. And believe it or not, I know him—or at least, I use to, years ago."

"Anyone I know?" Sheila asked.

"I don't know, it's Lamar Wilson. Tall, dark, handsome, you know the type."

"Never heard of him—but he sounds like he could fix up more than your house." Sheila raised her eyebrows up and down.

"Last I knew, he was married." Vanessa responded.

"So?" Sheila looked at her with incredulity. "Oh, I forgot. Not your style." She flapped her hand again and grabbed another slice of pizza.

"That's right." Confirmed Vanessa.

"All right. I'm initiating operation Sheila." I'm going to find you a man, girlfriend."

"Please don't. I'll be just fine chugging along on my own. " Vanessa finished her wine and they called it a night.

* * *

The following week, it was gym day. Vanessa's heart sped up in anticipation while walking to her car from work. When she came out of the dressing room it flip-flopped and skipped a beat when she saw Jim at the treadmill.

She walked over to the station beside him, smiled, and started the machine.

He smiled warmly at her, his dark eyes sparkling. "I've got something for you. "He handed her a small envelope and said, "I'm going over to the weights now. I look forward to your answer; which ever one it might be." He stopped his treadmill and walked away.

Vanessa slowed her pace and looked at the envelope. It was a lovely pastel peach. Written on the outside was: *Shy Lady*, with a curly sweep beneath.

With shaking fingers, Vanessa opened the envelope and pulled out an invitation card. What was written inside caught her breath, heat rose to her cheeks.

Dear, Shy Lady.

I would love the honor of dining with you. I was thinking of Mario's pizza. It's nothing fancy, but I like down to earth people, and down to earth food.

If you're inclined to spend a couple of hours with me, we can get to know each other a little.

If it's a yes, please walk over to the weights and tell me your name.

If it's a no, just keep on the treadmill. You and I can continue with friendly smiles and mutual workouts. I'll hope you change your mind one day, but I won't bother you. You'll always be beautiful.

With burning cheeks, not giving herself time to think and chicken out, Vanessa shut off her treadmill. She walked over to Jim and the weights. He looked up and stopped what he was doing.

She stuck out her slender hand and said, "Hi. My name's Vanessa.

*   *   *

Vanessa sat in her wicker chair. Her mama's rosebush, blushing its pink tender blossoms, filled her heart.

Her date with Jim was the following weekend. She mentally went through her closet, wondering what to wear.

The phone rang, startling her back to present time. It was Sheila. She was hysterical.

"Oh, God, Vanessa. What am I going to do?" She broke down crying. Her following words were unintelligible.

Vanessa sat up in her chair. "Sheila? What's wrong? What's happened, are the kids okay?" She heard her friend take a deep breath and blow her nose.

"The kids are fine. They're all in bed. He knows, he found out, Nessa. I don't know what to do. He's going to divorce me."

Vanessa took a deep steadying breath. She'd never seen her friend come remotely close to being upset, let alone hysterical. "Okay, slow down and tell me what happened."

"I came home, and found Steven gone. There was a note on the table. It said he saw my car outside the motel. He said he needs time to think. He said he's going to talk to a lawyer about divorcing me."

"*Was* it your car? Can he be sure it was *your* car?" Vanessa tried furiously to think of a way out for her friend.

"Of course, he can be sure. You know my car. I've got those bumper stickers on the back." Sheila stopped, blew her nose, and sighed in Vanessa's ear. "I mean, yeah, Steven's a pain in my ass, but I do love him. What am I going to do?"

Vanessa knew it was wrong, but she cared about her friend. She'd met Sheila's kids; they were great and Sheila was great with them. Yes, she was wild, but Vanessa knew she loved her family.

"Listen. You need to calm down. We'll think of something. Something feasible that Steven will believe. I don't want you to lose your family." Vanessa thought for a minute. "Remember that doctor that came for a conference? You had to provide him with some of our records in the respiratory department, remember?"

"Yes, Dr. Wilcox." Sheila's voice held a sliver of hope.

"Well, what if you were there at the motel to drop off some papers for another doctor? Would Steven believe that? Does he know how long you were there?" Vanessa felt a mixture of excitement and disgust with herself. It was disquieting. This wasn't like her.

"Oh, my, God. That's genius, Nessa. It just might work." Sheila shouted.

"All right. Take a few minutes to work out a story, and a doctor's name. Then, call your husband. Save your marriage, girl. I know you love your family." Vanessa hesitated. "But I'm telling you, this goes against every grain in my body. You need to stop all this running around. You need to prove to Steven you're worthy of him and your kids."

"I know, you're right. Thanks so much, my friend."

Exhausted, Vanessa got up, went into the house, and washed her wine glass. She hadn't told Sheila about her upcoming date with Jim. It wasn't the right time. She loved her friendship with Sheila, but Vanessa felt a little soiled in her heart when she took herself off to bed.

*　　*　　*

Dressed in jeans that accented her slim hips, Vanessa tugged at her blue and white top. She walked through the Italian restaurant door and spotted Jim right away.

He stood and waved her over to the table. "Vanessa, your name is as beautiful as you are."

She breathed a sigh of relief when she saw that, indeed, the restaurant atmosphere and its people were down to earth.

She'd giggled after the third time she'd caught him trying to hide his dirty fingernails. Surprising herself, Vanessa had gently took his hands in hers, and said, "Don't worry about that. You've told me you're a mechanic. I respect hardworking men."

Jim flashed a brilliant smile that started in his eyes and moved down to his mouth. "Nevertheless. I will definitely search for a solution to my work grime."

After dinner, Jim walked her to her car, then asked, "So, do you think you may want to do this again?"

"I'd love that. I had a really good time." She hesitated, then smiled. "I feel very comfortable with you."

"That's the best news I've had since you accepted my invitation. I'd love to do it next week, but I have to go to Ohio. My uncle passed and I need to help my aunt with clearing up his affairs. I'm not sure how long I'll be gone."

Vanessa's heart dropped. This was all a little too familiar.

Jim must have seen it, he said, "I will be back. I've got my business, and I can only trust the manager to run it for me for so long." He lifted her chin with his index finger. "I may be completely off the mark here, but I feel like we're two peas in a pod."

Vanessa drove home with a warm feeling in her heart. Jim was a very nice gentleman—a man's man. But she was going to take this one slow. Her heart was still tender from the last break.

Because these insects require stable oxygen levels and clean water, scientists consider them reliable bio indicators of the health of an ecosystem.

9

Vanessa walked in her front door, dropped her purse on the couch and flopped beside a barking Bella.

"Hey, girl. I had dinner with a very nice man tonight." She stroked the top of her Yorkie's head. "I want to do it again, and so does he. But he has to go out of town—out of state, actually. Ohio."

Vanessa got up from the couch and started to disrobe. She turned back to Bella who sat on the cushion with her ears pricked and her head tilted to the side.

"Kind of sounds familiar, doesn't it?" She sighed. "Well, it's a wait and see, anyway. I really hope it works out, but we're not setting ourselves up like last time, are we, girl?"

Bella, gave her a little snouty bark in answer.

Vanessa laughed, patted her baby's head, and went to bed.

The next morning at work, she was in a decent mood.

"What's up, short stuff?" John mused when she entered the records room.

"What's up, yourself, John? You know, you're not exactly a tall drink of water." Vanessa chided back.

"True, true. But honey, what's in this small package is dynamite." He flashed her his brilliant white grin.

"You're too much for me, darlin'. I'm off to earn my wages." Vanessa went out the door to get her equipment set up for rounds. Her spirits lifted even more when she saw Mr. Smith was on her schedule today. She wouldn't have to make an excuse to go see him.

"Hey there, handsome. Long time no see." Vanessa wheeled her cart into her favorite patient's room.

"Well now, is it Ms. Snapdragon, or Ms. Dragonfly today?" Mr. Smith said from his wheelchair.

"Oh, I guess it's a little bit of both this morning." She chuckled and unhooked her hoses.

"Regardless, young lady, you just put me through your torture last Friday. Although, I must admit, it's been a long weekend without your sparkling eyes." His laugh turned into a cough.

Vanessa pulled his arms above his head to open his air passage. When his coughing fit subsided, she talked soothingly to him throughout his entire treatment.

*   *   *

Sheila caught up with her outside of work that afternoon. "Hey, girl. You're coming with me for drinks. I won't take no for an answer." She grabbed Vanessa's arm and led her to her car.

"Our girls' night out is Thursday, Sheila." Vanessa protested.

"I gotta talk, and it can't wait until Thursday. So, you're coming with me to Sparks. I can't stay long; Steven is watching me like a hawk. He kind of believed my doctor's records story, but I guess he kind of didn't." Sheila opened Vanessa's car door for her and motioned her in. "Sparks, fifteen minutes, girlfriend. Do a sister a favor."

Vanessa laughed. "All right, you win. See ya there." She shut her door and cranked up her car.

They walked into Sparks together. Sheila was smiling ear to ear, and kept glancing at Vanessa.

"You seem to be in an awfully good mood for someone who wants to talk about her troubles." Vanessa ventured.

"Oh, I'll get through it. Come on." Sheila guided her to a table with a man sitting, sipping a drink.

He stood when they reached the table. "Wow. Is this the friend you told me about, Sheila? I'm impressed."

Sheila sat down, motioning for Vanessa to do the same.

Vanessa's mind raced furiously. *What the heck, Sheila. No. Really, what the hell?*

He was skinny, had a gold tooth, a goatee, a sharp chin, and nose. His eyes were a pretty amber, but she saw no kindness in them; they looked hungry, and not in a good way.

"Vanessa, this is Tony Putnam. Tony, this is my friend, Vanessa."

Tony stood and held out his hand. "Very pleased to meet you, Vanessa."

Reluctantly, Vanessa shook his hand, shivering inwardly. "Nice to meet you."

"What can I get you ladies to drink?" He motioned for a waiter.

They put their orders in and began small talk about work and weather; meaningless chatter that passed the time until their drinks arrived.

"Tony here is in commodities, Vanessa. Aren't you, Tony?"

The drinks arrived, including a fresh one for Tony. He paid the waiter, lifted his finger for him to wait, and downed the last half of his first cocktail. He put the empty glass, nothing but ice now, on the tray and dismissed him.

Sheila what have you gotten me in to?

Sheila's phone rang. "Excuse me." She answered it. "Oh, hi, Steven. Yes, I'm on my way. I stopped in at Sparks to have a quick drink with Vanessa." She listened. "Yes, I'm on my way out the door right now. Do you need me to pick anything up, honey?" She waited. "Okay, great. I'll see you in twenty." She hung up.

Sheila took two gulps of her drink and turned to Vanessa. "I swear to God, that man is driving me crazy. He keeps track of my every move." She took another gulp. "Well, gotta go." She got her purse and sashayed out the door.

Vanessa remembered to close her mouth. She knew her cheeks were burning, fueled by the anger at her friend for putting her in this situation.

"Looks like we're left here by our little old lonesome selves," said Tony with his hungry eyes.

She didn't like those eyes. She thought his looks were feral, but most of all she didn't like those eyes. She didn't like him.

Vanessa was raised and bred with politeness from her mother, as well as her grandmother. So it went against every grain in her body when she stood and said, "I apologize, Tony. But I really must go. I've never cared for false pretenses, no matter who lays them at my feet. Best wishes on your future endeavors." She smiled at his open-mouthed astonishment, pushed back her chair, and left the restaurant.

*   *   *

Her house phone was ringing when she walked in the door. She ran to pick it up. It was Jim. She couldn't help but smile in spite of the anger at her unpleasant afternoon.

"Hi, Jim. Did you make it? How was your trip?"

"I did. The trip wasn't bad; a little traffic through Cincinnati, since I hit it around rush hour, but otherwise it was smooth sailing."

She was soothed by the sound of his warm deep voice, and his casual manner of speaking. He wasn't on the make like Daryl had been. Jim was genuine.

"That's great to hear. Any idea what's ahead? What you'll need to do for your aunt?"

"Not yet. I just thought I'd call and let you know I got here safe and sound. It'll probably take me a few days, maybe a week, just to sort out what needs to be done. But I'll keep you posted." She heard something like the mouth piece being covered. Then, he came back on. "Vanessa, my aunt needs me. I've got to go. You take care and keep our next dinner in mind, okay?"

"Okay, Jim. I'm looking forward to it. And please give your aunt my condolences."

Vanessa's heart fluttered a little in anticipation. She looked around her living room; the floor in front of her bathroom door. It was sunken. Her couch was threadbare.

For goodness sakes, my house reflects the way I've felt for the past few months. What will Jim think? She put her hands on her hips. *Well, I don't feel that way anymore.* "I'm doing something about this right now."

She picked her phone back up, looked in the drawer for the number her cousin, Michael, had given her, and dialed it.

"Here goes nothing."

"Hello?" A female voice answered.

"Oh, hi. My name's Vanessa Graham. I was looking for Lamar? I was told he could do renovation work on my home?"

"Yes, hold on."

Vanessa heard a loud bray—"Laaammmaaaaar!" in the background. There was a clunk, then the phone was silent.

Oh my gosh. Did she hang up on me?

"Hello? Hello." She was about to hang up.

"Hello, this is Lamar."

"Hi, Lamar, this is Vanessa Graham. My cousin, Michael, gave me your number. He said you do repairs on houses?"

"Oh, hey. Yeah, I sure do. I waved at you in the parking lot the other week. How are ya? You need some repairs done? When can I come out and look at everything?"

Wow, this is going fast.

"Um, sure. How about Thurs—" she thought about her girls' night out with Sheila. Mad or not—she'd keep that date with her friend. "How about Friday evening at 5?"

"I'll be there with bells on."

In various spiritual pathways, the
dragonfly acts as a messenger
between the worlds.

10

Vanessa opened the door at Sheila's knock. "Hi," she said, then, turned around and went into the kitchen.

"Well, that's a fine, 'how do ya do?' What's up? I don't even smell tacos." She followed Vanessa to the kitchen and sat at the table.

"Nope, no tacos. There're hot dogs. Plain old hot dogs, and I'm not sure I should let you have any of them."

"What'd I do?"

Vanessa put her hands on her hips and cleared her throat. "Tony? Really? Do I look like I enjoy the company of a sleaze?"

"Oh, that. Well, I told you I'd find you somebody. Tony's a nice guy, he's not a sleaze. I was only trying to help." She looked at Vanessa with wide-eyed innocence.

"Oh, forget it." Vanessa flapped her hand. "Just don't ever try to help me again. I'll take care of myself. Deal?"

"Deal. And frankly, hot dogs sound great. Pun intended. Let's eat!"

They had finished their dinner and were in Vanessa's rose garden when Sheila's phone rang.

"Hey, Steven. I'm here with Vanessa. We had hot dogs."

She listened.

Vanessa could hear his voice booming through Sheila's phone.

Tears came to Sheila's eyes.

"But, Steven. I don't even know that kid, Donnie said—"

Vanessa heard his voice clearly. *That's the point Sheila. You don't know who your 13-year-old son hangs out with.'*

"Look, I'll meet you at the station in twenty minutes. We can discuss all this when we get our boy home." Sheila hung up, hung her head, and broke down crying.

When her sobs subsided, she took a deep breath, reached for her wine, and put it down again. "I don't need any more of that; I've got to go to the police station. Donnie was arrested for stealing." She spat the last word. "Stealing, Vanessa." Her eyes shot angry sparks at her friend.

"He's been hanging out with that one boy, Tommy. I didn't know he was a bad character. Steven says its all my fault. I'm not home enough to know what my kids are doing." She punched her thigh with a closed fist. "And he's right. Damn it, Nessa, he's right."

Vanessa helped her friend clean herself up, filled her a coffee to go, and sent her on her way.

She stood in the doorway watching her friend drive away. "My poor, sweet friend. What am I going to do with you?"

*   *   *

Friday after work Vanessa scurried around to tidy up. Dirty dishes soaked in the sink from her dinner with Sheila from the night before.

She closed the door to her bedroom. *I'll get to that later.* She heard a vehicle pull up, glanced at her watch, it was right on 5:00 p.m.. "Well, he's punctual, I'll give him that."

Vanessa looked out the window and saw a white pick-up park in her drive. A tall slim man got out and walked toward her front door.

She went to the door and opened it before he could knock. "Hi, Lamar. Thanks for coming over."

"Not a problem. Nice to see you." He nodded once.

She stepped back, pulled the door wide so he could enter. "Would you like coffee or tea?"

"No, thanks. I've got another appointment to get to after this."

He seemed aloof to Vanessa, but she didn't miss him eyeing her up and down. It gave her a tingle down her spine. She glanced at his left hand and didn't see a wedding ring. *I wonder who that woman was that answered his phone.*

"Well," she said. "Let's get to it then."

She took him around the house, showing him the walls that needed painting, floorboards needing repair, or to be replaced, and her kitchen cabinets.

"I really love my cabinets. I don't want to replace them, but I'm not sure you'll be able to repair the damages."

"Oh, that's not a problem. You can keep these. I'll be able to make them almost like new," he said confidently.

"Is it too much for you to do by yourself? I realize it's a lot of work." Vanessa ventured.

"Oh, no ma'am. I can handle it. It depends on when you want it finished. For big jobs, I bring in a helper. But there is not a job that I can't handle by myself." Lamar raised his eye brows twice and winked with a lop-sided grin. "And I'm sure I'd enjoy this one."

Vanessa's face flushed with heat. "Oh, well, that's great. I like your confidence. Will you take the job?"

"Let me go home and write up an estimate for you. I'll get it to you tomorrow. Is that good?"

"Yes." She breathed a sigh of relief. "That's fine. I'm so glad I'm finally doing something about my poor house. It's been neglected for such a long time."

"Well, now. Leaving something neglected is never a good thing. We'll have to see to that." His eyes roamed over her body again, his crooked grin in place. He tipped two fingers to his fore-head in a salute and said, "Until tomorrow then."

He can't be married; not with those looks he gave me. Well, gave my body, actually. Never mind all that. You've got Jim, and that guy at the meat counter. She shook her head. "Girl, you're starting to sound like Sheila." She shook her head again and laughed. "No, way."

Vanessa went to the gym on Saturday. She figured the day wouldn't matter since Jim was out of town, anyway.

After a vigorous workout, she decided to stop by the store and pick up some pork chops for dinner.

She walked up to the meat counter and eyed the selections. She was thinking of a double chop, stuffed with an apple and onion dressing.

His smooth voice sounded above her bent head. "Hey there, pretty lady. Can I help you find something?"

Startled, she looked up into Robert's eyes and smiled. Her heart skipped. It was his voice more than his eyes that got to her.

"I was thinking–" She'd lost her train of thought and scrambled desperately to get it back. "Um . . . I was thinking of stuffed double pork chops."

"I can hook you up with that. I'll need to cut 'em fresh for you. In fact, I can cut enough for two if you invite me to dinner. I'm free this evening and your meal sounds as delicious as you look."

Vanessa's cheeks were burning and her heart raced. *Am I ready for something like this? My house is still a mess.*

"I, uh . . . I'm—" She was going to say she wasn't prepared for company just yet when he interrupted with a chuckle.

"Tell you what. You think over your answer while I cut your chops." He smiled his big smile. "Be right back."

Vanessa stood there thinking. She could always explain that she was in the middle of renovations, but what about Jim? They really weren't an item yet.

Robert returned with the white wax paper package. He held it out to her with his left hand.

There was a ring on it.

Vanessa's mouth dropped open. Her heart sank with sadness, then filled with anger. *How low can you go? This jerk is married. Maybe I should invite his wife to come along.* She snatched the package from him, said, "Thank you," and walked away.

11

Vanessa slept fitfully all through the night. Her dreams were filled with images of her phone tryst with Daryl; Of her swooning at his actions of treating her like a princess—then Daryl's face morphing into Robert's. He turned around, held up his left hand with the wedding ring on it and burst out laughing—pointing at her laughing his maniacal laugh.

She woke, groggy and unrested. After her shower, she dressed in her uniform, looked at herself in the mirror. *That's about enough of that. Every man on this earth is not out to get me. I refuse to let my bad decisions haunt my future happiness. Besides, Robert wasn't even a decision. I stopped that crap.* Aloud she said "Let that shit go, girl. You're better than all of 'em."

Vanessa walked into records with a smile on her face. "Good morning, John."

"Morning, Glory. You look full of yourself today." He raised his eyebrows suggestively.

"I *am* full of myself, John. And happily so," Vanessa retorted. "Hi, Susan."

"Hi, Vanessa. You'll be glad to know Mr. Smith had a good night last night. So he's on your schedule again today."

"Well, you can go on up and give Mr. Smith some of your happily so." John made quotations with his fingers.

"You're just jealous. But I tell you, if you were in Mr. Smith's place, I'd give you just as much attention, Mr. John Hawkins. And be sure, I'd drop the Mr., you're undeserving.

They all laughed. Vanessa grabbed her clipboard and went to get her machines ready.

Vanessa entered Mr. Smith's room to find a stately slender woman sitting in the chair beside a sleeping Mr. Smith.

A thick book lay in her lap. She turned to Vanessa with a gentle smile and put her finger to her lips. Her silver hair gleamed in sunlight, mimicking the strand of pearls adorning her throat.

Vanessa nodded, pointed to her watch, and mouthed, 'later'. She quietly turned her cart around and went to the next patient on the schedule.

She went up to the nurses' station and asked, "Mr. Smith's allowed to sleep in the morning?"

The head nurse chuckled. "The General insisted on it."

"The General?" Vanessa asked.

"Oh, yes. Mrs. Smith," said the nurse.

"*That's* who that lovely lady is." Vanessa smiled and folded her arms over her chest.

"Lovely she is, but made of steel. We're just foot soldiers that do her bidding when she's here. That woman has an iron will when it comes to protecting her husband."

"Well, bless her, then. I think that kind hearted old man needs a bit of steel to look out for him." Vanessa laughed. "I'll be back later."

After dinner, Jim called with news that he'd be stuck in Ohio a while longer.

"Uncle Herman left so much undone. I can't find any documents pertinent to the mortgage, the note on the car, the lawnmower, Aunt Ada's sure he still owed money on that," Jim commiserated.

"Goodness. It's a good thing you're there to help her, Jim. You must be a God send." Vanessa's heart went out to him. He sounded so defeated and tired.

"Well, I'm glad to be here for her. So, how are you?"

"I'm fine. I met such a regal lady today. Well, I didn't really meet her, but we exchanged a silent moment." Vanessa recalled the dark liquid eyes full of fierce love for her husband, and gentle kindness for Vanessa. She wondered if Mr. Smith had spoken of her to his wife.

"It sounds like she made an impression on you," Jim ventured.

"She did. She reminded me of my mother. Sometimes I really wish she were here with me. You know, through the bad times." Vanessa thought of all the tough times she went through being a single mother. She didn't know if she could have made it if not for the strength and guiding love of her mom.

"Times have been tough?" Jim asked.

"They were. I raised my son on my own. My ex-husband was a closet gambler. He'd buy things like a big screen TV for himself, and a $1,400 Rive Gauche tote bag for me, saying it was from a bonus from work. Then his bookie called for money." Vanessa chuckled softly. I found out he was unfaithful after . . . well, let's just say I found out. That's something I'll never tolerate. But I can say my son is all the better for it. He graduated, has a great job, his own family. I couldn't be more proud."

"I'd love the honor of meeting him one day. But I must say, I'm not surprised. You're a wonderful woman, Vanessa. You may underestimate yourself at times." Jim chuckled.

"I've had some rough times myself. I'd have to say I've fashioned myself after Uncle Herman. My dad passed when I was a kid. He was there for me when my wife passed." He sighed. "But, I'm all the stronger for it."

"Yes. Life does make us stronger on our way through all the lessons there are for us." Vanessa's eyes teared up. "I miss you, Jim. I'd like to get to know you better in person. Not just on the phone."

"And I miss you, shy lady. We'll have our time. For now, though, I must bid you a good night. I've got to cook dinner for Aunt Ada; she's not doing too well."

"Well, bless you, Jim. You take care of that good lady."

The more Vanessa got to know him, the more fond of him she became; and the more she yearned for his companionship, any companionship.

As promised, Lamar and his helper were in her driveway fifteen minutes before she left for work.

She opened the front door, waved them in, and said, "I see you brought your own coffee." She put her hands on her hips, "Okay, so where do we start?"

"Well, good morning, fine lady. This is my assistant, Adam. Adam, this is Miss Graham." Lamar made introductions.

Vanessa eyed the young man. Her heart went out to him. His greasy blonde hair hung in his eyes. Pimples dotted his face; some appeared about to pop. *Well, his clothes are clean, at least.*

Adam flushed and nodded. "Nice to meet you, Ms.—"

"Vanessa is fine, Adam. It's nice to meet you." She stuck out her hand for him to shake.

Adam turned an even deeper red down to his neck. "Yes, ma'am, Miss Vanessa. It's nice to meet you." He shook her hand.

Lamar walked through her home showing her the floor boards he would pull up, explaining he'd need to pull up the carpet. He asked if she'd like him to clean it before laying it back when the boards were replaced.

"Oh, goodness, no. Toss that filthy thing outside. If you could haul it away for me, please do that." She chuckled.

"Ah, I see. A whole new fresh start." Lamar hooked his thumbs into the front of his belt.

"Yes. Exactly. I'll leave you to it, then." She started past him to the door.

"Yes'm. Just leave me to it," said Lamar, and winked at her.

Fishermen used them as an indicator of good fishing grounds. Plenty of dragonflies meant there were plenty of fish around.

12

*H*er ratty carpet was rolled up and sitting in the back of Lamar's pick up when Vanessa pulled up to her house after work.

"Good bye you nasty old thing." She laughed out loud.

She got out of her car and forced herself to walk, overcoming the urge to run in her excitement to see the progress.

The floorboards were all in place. She could barely tell the difference between the old and the new. Lamar had matched them so skillfully.

He looked up from where he knelt and smiled. "Welcome home. What d'ya think?" He stood. "Adam, carry those old boards out to the truck. I'll finish the pick-up in here."

"Yes, sir, Mr. Lamar." He nodded at Vanessa. "Afternoon, ma'am." Adam picked up the boards and left.

"What do I think? It's fantastic." Vanessa beamed.

"I figured you can have me refinish this floor, or you can buy another carpet. I can lay it for ya."

Vanessa looked at her floor. "I'll have to think on that a minute. I don't know how to thank you. It looks amazing."

"Well, some advance money would be a good start." He rubbed his hand over his shiny pate and smiled at her sheepishly.

"Oh, my. Of course. How stupid of me. How much would be good?" Her face felt hot. She reached for the checkbook in her purse and fumbled it out; uncomfortable from his manner. *Was that crass or am I just embarrassed.*

"I guess five oughta do us for a while." He leaned down and started picking up their tools.

Vanessa handed him the check saying, "Thank you, so much. I really do love it."

"Oh yeah. You're gonna love it all. I guarantee it." He tipped her a wink, and saluted with two fingers. "Bright and early in the morning?"

She smiled. "Bright and early."

*   *   *

"Oh my gosh. How long has this man been at it? Your house looks great." Sheila turned in a circle.

"Well, except for that couch. Your floor is beautiful. Who knew what was underneath that carpet?"

"Lamar refinished the floor for me," Vanessa said proudly.

"And that rug is to die for—but that couch." Sheila shook her head.

"I'm replacing that next week. I just need to find one that I want. Lamar will pick it up for me. I want something that picks up the light sage colors in the rug." Vanessa walked into the kitchen. "Let's eat. I'm starving."

"I'll pour the wine," Sheila volunteered.

They took their wine outside after dinner.

"How's your love life?" Sheila plopped into her regular chair.

"Non-existent," replied Vanessa. "The guy I'm interested in went to Ohio to help his aunt with his uncle's affairs after he passed. He's really a great guy."

"How's the action?" Sheila raised her eyebrows up and down.

Vanessa leveled a glare at her friend.

"Okay, fine. You have no idea. After all, it was only a," she made quotations, "first date." Sheila sipped her wine.

"Come on, Nessa. There're a million fish in the sea."

Vanessa set her glass on the table and leaned forward. "What you don't understand, my friend, is that I'm not interested in a million fish. I want something meaningful. One special guy that will sit at my table and help pull the load. A partner in companionship. Someone with whom I can share a mutual respect."

She drank some wine. "That's what's important to me. If great sex becomes a part of the package— all the more rich."

"I hear ya. I hear ya, and hear ya. I'm telling you I've *got* that, and it's no walk in the park.

I've got Donnie on probation—which Steven blames me for. So, I have to listen unendingly to his whining complaints." Sheila shook her head.

"Is Steven still going on about your car outside the motel room?"

"Ah, hell no, girl. I got all that handled." She flapped her hand.

"And in Donnie's case, I just went on about a weak father figure," here her voice became wheedling, "but that's okay, I love you anyway, baby."

She sipped her wine and laughed. "Then, one hell of a romp in the sack and I've wrapped him up all over again." She held up her pinky finger.

A wave of pity ran through Vanessa for Steven. He really was a nice guy, and from what she had seen and heard a great father.

"Hcy, tell me about this handyman carpenter you got sprucing up the place. I may want a little work done, myself." Sheila giggled.

"Well, he's not great looking, but not really bad looking. He's bald, wears glasses, his upper body's pretty toned, I guess from the carpentry work he does. He *can* be a little crass."

"He doesn't sound like too much of anything. Good toned upper body, and crassness are okay—that part sounds like my style," Sheila said.

Vanessa thought it through, she recalled the shiver that went through her when he eyed her up and down and said, 'Nothing does well when neglected, we'll have to see about that.'

She said, "Oh, I don't know. I kind of find him charming for some reason."

Vanessa didn't know why she felt compelled to defend a man she hardly knew. Nonetheless, her heart had developed a small soft spot for him.

*   *   *

It was couch hunting day. Vanessa had walked through three furniture stores in search of something that caught her eye.

On her way to the fourth and last store she commiserated at possibly having to go to a larger town for her search. *Come to that, I need to find a new grocery store. I will not subject myself to*

Robert's insinuating advances, nor put myself in a position where I'm required to give him an explanation.

She pulled into the parking lot of her last-hope store.

The salesman walked up to her and offered help.

"Well," she said, "I've walked miles of furniture store floors and my feet are aching. Maybe you can help me out with that.

"I'm looking for a couch—maybe even a matching chair. I have an oriental floral rug and I'd love to be able to find a light sage that brings out the rugs colors."

"Let me see, I believe we may have something right up your alley. We got a few new items in last week's shipment." He turned to her, "Is cloth okay? I don't think you'll find much of your color scheme in leather."

"No, no, I prefer cloth." Vanessa nodded.

"Great, come this way. We have a spray guard to protect the material from stains."

Vanessa followed him around the corner of furniture and stopped in her tracks. A beautiful plush sofa and chair sat together that were the perfect color.

"I want those," she said with an awestruck sigh.

At the payment counter, the salesman handed her the receipt.

"You've been so helpful. I wonder, would you know of a grocery store that can cut fresh meat, special cuts? One that has a butcher?"

"Oh yes, Martin's Meats and Groceries."

"Well, that's where I always went, but," she hesitated, "I had an encounter that made me uncomfortable, and—"

The salesman's brows shot up. "I think I understand. The butcher they had there?" He looked at her questioningly.

"Yes, exactly," Vanessa confirmed.

"Well, not to worry. I know the owner, and Robert's been fired. Mr. Martin told me so over drinks last weekend." He put his hand to the side of his mouth as though imparting a secret. "Sexual harassment of a customer. And not just one customer. There were a number of complaints."

Vanessa drove home on a cloud of relief and excitement. *Perfect new couch and chair, and I get to keep shopping at my favorite store.*

"Each day can be bright and new if I want it to be."

American Indians believe red dragonflies can bring a time of rejuvenation after a long period of trials and hardship.

13

Vanessa pulled into her driveway and saw her old couch in the back of Lamar's pickup. Adam was putting their tools in the bed.

She got out of her car, grabbed her purse, and slammed the door shut in her excitement.

"My new couch is here?" she asked Adam.

"Yes, ma'am, Miss Vanessa. We carried it in not an hour ago." His smile was sweet.

She reached out and touched his shoulder on the way by. She silently cringed at the smell of his sour sweat. *Oh, honey you're such a nice boy, but please bathe. I need to talk to him one of these days. Some poor kids just aren't taught any better.*

"Well, I'm going to see it. I can't wait." She called over her shoulder.

She walked in the door and gasped softly. There were her sofa and chair. They were the perfect color; light sage to bring out the lighter greenery in her oriental rug.

She heard the toilet flush. Then Lamar came out of the bathroom, hitching up his paint stained jeans.

His grin grew wide, then bloomed into a full out smile. She'd never noticed how large his teeth were before. The gap between his front teeth had always been there; but his teeth were uncommonly long. His eyes sparkled at seeing her joy.

"I love it, Lamar. Isn't it beautiful?" She pranced over and sat on the couch. She leaned back, and sighed deeply.

"Aah. My gosh, it's perfect." She jumped up, went to the chair, and settled in.

All the while, Lamar watched her. She caught his look; he was hungrily eyeing her up and down. Vanessa realized she was making a spectacle of herself and quickly stood up.

"Thank you so much, for getting it for me." She ran her hand over the material. "I really appreciate it."

Adam had come back into the house. "Ma'am? I was wondering if you minded if I could keep your old couch. I'm kinda sittin' on orange crates with cushions on 'em."

"Of course, I don't mind, Adam. I was just going to ask Lamar if he would take it to the dump for me." She smiled.

"Well, that saves some money, then. I'll just need the gas money it took me to go pick it up." He turned to Vanessa. "I'll only need $50 for that. I've got a guzzler out there."

Vanessa was taken aback, but had the where-with-all not to let her mouth drop open.

"Of course. No problem. I'll have to write you another check. I don't have cash." She reached down to the couch for her purse.

"Um. Okay, but better make it $60 instead, I'll have to go by your bank."

*   *   *

Vanessa had three days before it was girl's night out with Sheila. She couldn't wait to show her friend the new purchases and the progress Lamar and Adam had made.

She decided to hop in her car and find some new draperies to go with her rug and couch. She could grab something quick to eat on her way back.

When she returned, her home phone was ringing. It was Jim.

She told him all about her new purchases and the work being done at the house.

He brought her up to date on his aunt's affairs, ending by saying, "A fifty-five-year marriage can accumulate a lot of paperwork, and loose ends," he paused. Then added, "I hope I'm not being too assumptive, Vanessa, but that's exactly what I want." He chuckled. "Without the loose ends, of course."

I . . . I guess that's what I've always wanted, Jim. But . . ." Her voice trailed away.

"I know you've been hurt in the past. In a way, I'm kind of glad. Elsewise I wouldn't have the blessing of getting to know you. But, I'm a one-woman man. I always have been. I'll let you sleep on that. Goodnight, beautiful lady."

*   *   *

Vanessa came home to find Lamar and Adam on her front porch hammering away at new floor boards.

"Oh," she said, walking up to them. "Is this going to take long? I have a friend coming for dinner."

"Nope. We'll be wrapping it up in ten minutes or less." Lamar stood aside to let her pass.

"Great. She's not due for another two hours." She went into the house, but not before she heard Lamar say, "She, huh?"

Vanessa changed her clothes and started for the kitchen to start prepping for dinner. It was taco night again. She heard voices outside the front door and thought at first that it was Lamar and Adam. Then she heard a woman's laugh, and recognized it immediately.

She went to the door and opened it. There stood Lamar with eyes agog.

Sheila was dressed to kill. Her midcalf skirt was slit up the side to reveal her entire thigh. Her off the shoulder blouse was cut so low it would have shown her cleavage vulgarly, if she'd had any.

Sheila giggled and waved her fingers at her. "Hey, there, Nessa. I thought I'd come early and let someone give me a tour of all the progress." She flicked her eyes at Lamar and tucked a non-existent hair on her forehead back in place.

"Well," said Vanessa. "You might as well come in and help me prep for dinner first. I'll give you the grand tour when it's done."

"Okay." She climbed a step making sure she led with the slit side first to reveal as much as possible.

"Lamar, is it?" Sheila inquired.

"Yes, ma'am." He did his two-finger salute and winked. "At your service."

"Will you be staying for dinner, too? We could use some male company."

Vanessa was embarrassed and sickened by her friend's outrageous flirtations. She said, "We'll be just fine. Now get in here and help me."

She could see Lamar chuckle silently. Then, he said, "That's all right, I gotta take my boy, Adam here home."

He looked at Adam. "Pick 'em up and let's go. We're good for the day."

He turned back to Sheila and said, "Thanks for the invite. Maybe another time." He bowed at the waist to them both. "You ladies have a nice night."

The Japanese consider red dragonflies to be "very sacred," offering a symbol of courage, strength and happiness.

14

I can't believe you." Vanessa turned and faced Sheila after closing the door on Lamar's retreating truck.

"What? You mean inviting that man to dinner?" Sheila asked incredulously.

"Yes, I mean inviting that man to dinner." Vanessa shook her head. "I mean, I've seen you in action before, but for God sakes, Sheila. You're shameless."

"Well, honey, I know how to flirt, and something needs jump starting here. He may not be much to look at, but did you see that package?" Sheila flopped her hand side to side, fingers flayed, as though cooling off burnt fingers.

"You're ridiculous." Vanessa blushed, and chuckled.

"Never mind. Look at that couch and chair. They're perfect. Classy, elegant, and comforting, just like you." Sheila sat in the chair. "Let's eat in here."

"No way. I wouldn't let you eat in here with my old stuff. What on earth makes you think I'd let you eat in here with the new?" Vanessa pulled her friend to her feet. "Come on. Since you're here this early, you're helping me cook."

After dinner and drinks, Sheila's parting comment played over and over in her mind the next few weeks. "You better get you some of that, or I *will*."

Over the next few weeks Lamar showed up without Adam more often than not. If she asked after Adam, all he'd say was, "Not here today."

As a result, Lamar stayed later and later to get to the point he needed before calling it a day.

Vanessa surreptitiously watched him. He was thorough and meticulous. She watched his arm and back muscles as he labored shirtless, carrying planks that were to replace her damaged ones.

Sheila's remark floated around in her thoughts. *Maybe it wouldn't be such a bad thing* to *invite him for dinner one evening.* Vanessa didn't like the idea of Sheila having a meaningless affair with someone she was gaining a bit of respect for.

He's the sole reason I'm so much happier in my home. It's cozy and it is *elegant.*

Toward the end of the second week, Lamar once again came without Adam. He was working on the cabinets in the kitchen.

Vanessa came home from work, greeting him, and went to change clothes.

She stood in front of the mirror and assessed what she'd chosen to wear: silky slacks that hugged her hips and hung loosely to her sandals; her top was high collared, baring her shoulders, with sleeves that mimicked the loose legs of her slacks.

She thought of Sheila's getup the other week and thought. *Polar opposites. I am elegant, aren't I?*

Vanessa smiled to herself. Then she thought of Jim. *What* the heck am I doing? This isn't me. She changed into blue jeans and a t-shirt and went out to the kitchen.

"Those cabinets are starting to look really good." She said, pouring herself a glass of wine.

"I'll have them looking like new in a few days." He turned to look at her, saw her glass of wine and raised his brow. "Say, I'm about to knock off, mind if I have one of those with you?"

"Sure." Vanessa rose and got him a glass, slightly taken aback at his boldness.

"Thanks." He poured himself a full glass up to the rim. "Cheers." He said and downed almost half of it.

"I really needed that. I'm a little out of sorts the past couple of days. I hope it doesn't show in my work."

"Your work is great, Lamar."

"Thanks. It's just . . . I got trouble at home is all." He shook his head.

He saw her glance at his ringless left hand. "Oh, yeah. I'm married, sort of." He held up his hand. "Job hazard, it catches on too much." He took a swallow of wine. "Truth is, it doesn't mean much anymore. I hate going home every day. I just sit there and feel like a louse. I can't do anything right. All she does is complain, and tell me everything I did wrong." Tears had surfaced in his eyes.

Vanessa sat there, torn. On a very deep level, she didn't trust this man. But she didn't have a basis for that feeling. Here he was pouring his heart out to her. *Those are real tears.*

"Didn't your marriage work at some point? I mean, is there a way you could get back to that?" she asked.

He snorted a short laugh. "Our marriage was a lie from the very beginning. She told me she was pregnant, so I married her. Well the pregnancy never appeared. She said she'd lost it, but I just can't believe that anymore. She started asking for more money and more money. She just had to have this big house with acreage. She knew I couldn't afford it. I do nothing but work, work, work." He sighed.

"That sounds terrible, Lamar. I'm so sorry." She felt as though she could relate to some of his woes. She'd been treated poorly in her marriage, as well.

"Oh, hey. Don't get me wrong. I'm no saint. I made a mistake; a bad mistake. I had an affair." He saw her stiffen at this information.

He looked her straight in the eyes, the tears were there again. "I was just so lonely." His voice broke. "I needed to feel like I was important to somebody; *anybody*. My wife hasn't touched me in years. I knew it was wrong, but God help me—I needed to feel like a man." He said this last with force. "I was being emasculated at home. Hell, I still am, every damn day. That's why I've filed for divorce. She doesn't know it yet. I just don't want to be around the fireworks when she finds out. I've raised her three kids, already. I just can't do it anymore."

Vanessa reached over and put her hand on his shoulder. "You'll get through it. You're a strong man; I can tell." Then, the impulse hit her. "Why don't you pour us another glass of wine and I'll cook us something to eat."

"Hey, that'd be great. I can't remember the last time I had a home cooked meal. My wife doesn't cook."

That was the statement that touched her the most; that, and the fact they'd not had relations for so long. *That would drive a man to do about anything. Oh, this poor tortured soul.*

Dinner was filled with conversation a little

more pleasant. He made her laugh a few times. He could actually be quite nice to be around.

She walked him to the door and showed him out. He turned to her halfway to his truck and said, "Thanks for lending an ear. I really needed it. I'm sorry I burdened you with my troubles. I'll be back bright and early in the morning."

"Bright and early," she smiled. Vanessa watched his taillights disappear in the distance, and hoped that she'd done the right thing. *I hope just listening, gave him some peace.*

She went to bed feeling lighthearted. She'd helped someone in need. Jim hadn't crossed her mind all night.

*   *   *

Dragonflies are deaf. They have no ears or tympanum. They feel loud sounds in very low frequencies. Eighty percent of their information is from their eyes ,processed through 30,000 lenses.

15

*T*rue to his word, Lamar was there early the next morning. Adam was in tow, but he looked tired and dirtier than ever.

"Morning," said Vanessa. She walked out the front door to her car.

"Hey, leaving so early? I thought I might grab a coffee from you." Lamar pulled his toolbox out of the truck bed.

Vanessa glanced at her watch. "Sorry, I've got a stop to make on my way to work. I've cleaned my kitchen up and I have to go." She took a step toward her vehicle, then stopped and turned to him. "You usually bring your own coffee."

He grinned sheepishly. "Well, yeah, I usually do, but I'm runnin' a little low on cash. I wanted to talk to you about that after work."

Vanessa's mouth dropped open, then immediately closed. Torn between his heartfelt talk with her last evening, and his pathetically crass manner in extracting more money from her, she just didn't know what to think. *He already almost twice over his bid and only half done with what he bid on.*

She composed herself and said, "Well, that's the best time to talk over things like that. I'll see you this afternoon."

She got in her car and drove away.

*　　*　　*

Sheila had begged off their girl's night out dinner; She had a date.

By Saturday, Vanessa needed her friend, so she called.

"How was your date?" She asked.

"So, so. The man's a slug in bed, but I got a lobster dinner and drinks." Sheila laughed. "So, it wasn't a total loss."

"You amaze me. You'd think we were polar opposites, yet we're best friends. I don't get it." Vanessa marveled.

"You know the old saying. Opposites attract. What've you been up to?" She inquired.

"I took your advice and asked Lamar to dinner." Vanessa confessed.

"You did? How'd it go?" Sheila's voice sounded strangely cool.

"I felt sorry for him. He's married but getting a divorce. She's a total witch to him. He had an affair—his wife hasn't touched him in years. I don't know, my heart went out to him, so I asked him to stay for dinner." Vanessa thought back on their easy conversation. "Just dinner—we talked a good deal and then he went home."

"Well, aren't you the virtuous one." Sheila's voice dripped with sarcasm.

"Not really. I actually had some terrible thoughts about him the other day." Vanessa confided.

Sheila's voice perked up. "Oh, do tell, do tell. I love the juicy stuff."

"Well, he's always asking for money. And it's always in the most awkward, clumsy way. I feel kind of bad for being so critical, he seems nice enough, but that ear and those teeth."

Sheila giggled. "I've never seen such giant freckles on a nose before."

Vanessa sighed. "Oh, my God. We sound like a couple of teenagers making fun of the new boy in school. Those are probably damage from the sun. The man's a hard worker."

They fell silent for a while. Vanessa reflected on her past experiences, mistakes in judgement she'd made. She hadn't shared these things with anyone. *What the heck, I'm talking to my best friend.*

"You know, other men I've known were as handsome as could be and they turned out to be horrid users. My husband being one of them. I was so naïve, I didn't know he was running around until he gave me his disease, I was so embarrassed, so humiliated. I swore that'd never happen to me again. After that, it was protection all the way. Unless it was phone sex. That's what I had with that jerk that tried to scam me. And he was a major jerk, but, Sheila, . . . have you ever had phone sex? It was fantastic!"

"I like the real thing, girl—look, I gotta go play wife and mom for awhile. We'll pick this up later."

*　　*　　*

Vanessa pulled into her drive after work anxious to see the border fence that Lamar was to finish today. The wood pattern she'd chosen was perfect for her backyard rose garden. Her haven would be perfect.

His truck wasn't there. *I guess they're already gone for the day.*

She hurried through her house before taking the time to change out of her uniform.

She stepped out the back sliding glass door, holding her breath in anticipation.

Nothing.

The wood stood stacked up against the old fence. Absolutely nothing had been done. *I just gave him $600 yesterday. What did he do with it?*

She walked around the house and saw nothing different. Walking through her living room she marveled at the, rug, her sofa and chair, her new drapes that complimented the rug, and the perfect planks on her floor.

Well, the man does do good work. I'll give him that. He probably got caught up doing something like the shed outside.

She changed her clothes and went to the kitchen to get something to eat. *That leftover fried chicken sounds heavenly.*

She opened the fridge and rummaged through to find the container she'd put the chicken in.

"Where on earth?" Vanessa mumbled. She decided to settle for some potato salad and would think about something more substantial later.

She went to the cupboard by the sink to get a plate.

The sink contained the empty container of chicken. Crumbs were everywhere, a dirty plate with chicken bones and dried potato salad sat beneath it.

She held up the container to see how much was left. It was half empty.

"Four pieces of chicken and half of my potato salad. Good Lord."

She shook her head and sat at the table to snack. "Maybe things will be better when his divorce goes through." Knowing if he was hungry and she was home, she'd feed him. But just the same, something didn't quite feel right.

*   *   *

Vanessa walked into the records room to find John and Susan laughing heartily.

"What's so funny, you two?"

"Oh, hi, Vanessa. I was just telling John about Mr. Smith and his wife this morning." She giggled then snorted. It set all of them to laughing.

Vanessa calmed enough to ask. "Okay, what were they up to?" She couldn't imagine that regal lady, Mrs. Smith, doing anything so humorous as to cause this laughter.

"Well, Mr. Smith said, 'First thing I do when I get out of here is light up my cigar.' The look on Mrs. Smith's face was priceless. Then she said, 'You just—' Susan burst into merriment once again; not able to contain herself.

"I suppose none of you have any work to do." Sheila's voice, cold as ice, came from the doorway. She put her hands on her hips. "What's so funny anyway?"

She turned to Vanessa. "Filling them in on your latest escapades?"

Susan turned beet red. "I was just sharing a moment of Mr. Smith's fun this morning. It was good to see him in such high spirits."

"Well, I'm so glad one of our patients was able to provide you three with such a good time." She turned on her heel and left.

Vanessa, Susan, and John were left with mouths wide open.

John finally said, "I thought she was your friend?"

Vanessa picked up her patient schedule, looked at it, then at Susan and John. "So did I."

16

Over the next few days Vanessa went about her work with trepidation. She'd felt humiliation in front of her coworkers, they were her friends. But she was the one singled out, even though it was addressed to all three of them. *I was the one targeted, and by my best friend.*

She hadn't seen Sheila at work since the incident, and was very glad. She didn't know how they would react to each other.

Finally, on the third night, unable to eat dinner for her nerves, she broke down and called.

"Hi, Nessa, we still on for Thursday? I found a new pizza place I want to try." Sheila sounded cheerful and warm.

Vanessa was taken aback. *It's as though nothing at all happened.* "Uh, I guess." Her voice sounded weak to her own ears.

Then, she recalled the heat that had gone to her face with the remarks, "Filling them in on your latest escapades?"

Vanessa's backbone kicked in; her courage along with it. "Look, I don't know what the other day was all about. You come in and dis me in front of my coworkers and act like I'm just a lowly employee that you don't even know."

"Oh, come on. That was nothing. I guess I was carrying my troubles from home to work." Sheila chuckled.

Infuriated at her friend's nonchalance, Vanessa said, "Well, it wasn't nothing to me, Sheila. You hurt my feelings. You know my work ethics. It's like you deliberately set out to hurt me."

"Nessa, I'm sorry. It *was* wrong of me. I saw you guys having fun and I got jealous." She sighed. "Look, I'll be honest with you, you're my best friend. I'm having problems at work, I'm having problems at home. Admin is on my ass for reports that I haven't even started yet."

Vanessa heard shouting in the background.

"Boys! Cut it out," Sheila screamed into the background. Then to Vanessa, "I'm coming over. We need to talk, and I'm going crazy here." She hung up.

Vanessa sat in shock, then burst out laughing. "Oh, Sheila, Sheila, Sheila."

Fifteen minutes later, her friend knocked on the door. "It's open." Vanessa shouted from the kitchen. She'd gotten her appetite back with the apology and antics of her friend.

Sheila sat down at the table. "Hey, make me one of those." She pointed to the sandwich Vanessa was making.

"I really am sorry, Nessa. Donnie keeps getting into trouble and my load at work gets heavier every week." She took the plate Vanessa handed her.

"I mean, I know that's no excuse, but haven't you ever taken your anger out on someone else? You know, just so you feel better inside."

Vanessa thought a minute, then nodded. "Yes, but only on the one that deserved it."

"Of course, Miss Goodie Two Shoes. I should have known." Sheila smiled her mischievous smile. "Who was it?"

"My ex." Vanessa smiled back and giggled.

"What'd you do? Tell me." Sheila leaned forward chewing a bite of sandwich.

"Well, I found out he was cheating on me. And not just once. He was stringing three or four of them along. So, I tried to kick him out and he wouldn't leave. He kept saying, 'They don't mean anything baby, they're just flings. You're the one I love.'" Her voice had taken on a wheedling tone.

"So, one day a fly got in our house. I killed it, chopped it up and put it in his dinner that night."

"Oh my God, you didn't," Sheila exclaimed.

"Oh, yes I did. I also made sure there was one leg on his potatoes so he could see it. He found it halfway through the meal."

Vanessa burst out laughing.

"What'd he say?" Sheila asked around a mouthful of sandwich.

"He said, 'Oh, yuck, what is this?' I said, 'That's the leg of the fly I killed earlier.' And he said, 'well it's in my dinner.' So I nodded and said, 'Uh huh, so is the rest of him.'"

They both burst into gales of fresh laughter. When Vanessa gained enough control to speak, she said, "He bolted up from the table, went and threw some clothes in a bag and left. I haven't seen him since."

With their friendship repaired they said goodnight and reaffirmed their Thursday girl's night out date.

* * *

Vanessa pulled in her drive after work. Adam was busy with the tools in the back of the pick-up. His jeans were crusty. His hair hung in his eyes almost dripping grease.

Her heart went out to him. He was so tall she had to shield her eyes from the sun when she looked up at him.

"Hey, Adam."

"Hey, Miss Vanessa."

"Do you mind if I talk with you for a moment?"

"No, ma'am." He set his tools down in the bed of the pick-up.

"Let's go over to the porch and sit down." She led him over and sat on the steps.

"You're a very nice young man, Adam. And I'd really like to see you do well. It may be none of my business, but I feel a responsibility to anyone I could help."

He blushed. "Yes, ma'am."

"It would make a big difference in your appearance if you showered more often and washed your hair. Maybe even trim it so it doesn't hang in your face? I bet if you did that your acne will clear up in no time." She patted him on the shoulder.

"Do you have a girl?"

"No, ma'am."

Vanessa stood up. "Well, if you do those two things and wash your clothes after each time you wear them, I bet you *will* have one."

He brightened a little, stood up, and said, "Yes, ma'am."

"See you later." Vanessa walked into her house smiling.

She stopped short. On her coffee table sat a vase of beautiful flowers; lilies and hydrangeas. Dumbfounded, she just stood there and gazed at them.

Lamar came in from the back garden smiling. "I know I've been a little behind on my work lately. I figured I'd try and make up for it by giving a beautiful, patient lady, some beautiful flowers."

The Native Americans perceived dragonflies as the "souls of the dead." Seeing a dragonfly around a loved one's death signifies their soul taking form in the spirit of dragonfly. It offers the assurance their soul is free.

17

The flowers Lamar had given her were starting to wilt, but she was loathe to throw them away.

Vanessa felt a strange fondness for him. She saw the kindness he was capable of, and these days, that outweighed his occasional crassness. *Although he tends to be lazy, maybe that's because his home life is so miserable.*

When she *did* think of Jim, she longed for his kind sparkling eyes adoring her. But for the most part her mind was filled with work, Sheila's troubles, her beautiful home, and of course, Lamar.

Vanessa sat on her sofa with Bella on her lap. Paying no attention to the news on TV, she was taking in her surroundings. They weren't quite so new anymore—being a few months old—but her furniture, her rug, her drapes; everything filled her with a fresh new joy.

She heard a vehicle pull up into the drive.

"Who could that be, Bella?" She kissed her Yorkie on the head and turned to look out the window.

It was Lamar's truck. "What's he doing here? It's Saturday."

Without thinking about it, or even knowing why, she rushed into her bedroom to change her top and check her hair.

Vanessa opened her door after the second knock. Lamar stood there with his silly lopsided grin, his big front teeth hanging out.

"I just wanted to stop by to thank a lady for her kindness." He pulled his arm out from behind him to produce another bouquet.

"Oh, how beautiful, and what kindness would you be speaking of?"

She took the proffered flowers. "Come on in and sit down." Vanessa stepped back.

"Thanks." He sat down on her sofa. "Adam told me you had a little talk with him. I don't know what was said, but I *will* tell you his enthusiasm to do a good job has doubled. In fact, we finished one job a day early. And get this, he asked me to drop him off at the barber shop by his house yesterday; said he could walk home from there."

"That's wonderful news. I'm so glad. He really is a nice boy." Vanessa lifted her old flowers out of the vase and went to change the water for her new bouquet.

"I don't know what I'm going to do with you spoiling me with these flowers."

"You deserve it, Vanessa. I've never met anyone like you before. You're so kind to everyone. Not like my wife, or *any* one I know. You're beautiful in spirit, as much as your physical self." He sighed.

"I know you probably don't care, but I've been thinking about you a lot. I just can't seem to get you off my mind. I want to make a clean breast of it with you." He looked down, his face reddening. "You know, in case one day I might have a chance with you."

He raised his head and looked at her with tear glistened eyes. "I wasn't quite honest with you before. I hadn't really broken it off with my affair. I didn't want to hurt her, but she's become as bad as my wife with her negativity. I've broken it off for good now. I'm moving in with my mother. She needs my help anyway and I could use a break from paying rent on an apartment. Sally won't move out of the house and I still have to pay the mortgage."

Vanessa sat in the shock of information overload. Her heart went out to this pitiful man who was obviously hurting. But she felt as though a burden of responsibility had been placed on her.

She was torn.

"I don't know what to say. I'm sorry you're having to deal with all this. I . . ."

"I didn't mean to burden you. I'm sorry I was so forward with my feelings." Lamar stood abruptly. "I'll get out of your hair." He turned to go.

"Wait, Lamar. I didn't mean . . . I mean, why don't you stay for dinner. We'll have some wine." She smiled. "Just promise we can keep the conversation light." She chuckled.

A smile broke out on his face. "That's the best idea I've heard all week."

*   *   *

Sunday was a relaxed day. Vanessa did her wash, cleaned her house, and spoke to her son and grandkids on the phone. It was joyous to hear of their grades, their friends, and most of all her son's promotion at work.

This was usually the day Jim called her. She dreaded it. What if he's not able to leave his aunt; again.

All day her mind had been filled with thoughts of Lamar. She found herself vacillating between the positives and the negatives; more and more on the positives. After all, he was here. *He can be kind. Yes, he even seems like he can be a stand-up guy.*

The phone rang.

She picked up the receiver and answered. "I'm going out on a limb here and just saying, hi, Jim. How are things?"

"Um, well, I'm not Jim, but I can always change my name for a pretty lady like you."

"Oh, Lamar." Heat rose to her cheeks, "I apologize, I was expecting a call."

"No problem. It wasn't important. I'll talk to you later." He hung up.

Vanessa sighed heavily. *Well, that was abrupt.* She turned to Bella beside her on the couch. "What do you think he wanted?"

She picked the tiny Yorkie up from the sofa and cradled her in her lap.

The rest of the day was spent waiting and wondering. Restlessly, she spent her time fidgeting. Toward evening, Vanessa decided to spend some time with her mother's roses and a glass of wine. She needed to relax enough to take herself to bed and get rid of the ping ponging thoughts of Lamar and Jim.

No phone call came that night.

18

*J*im's call came the following Tuesday evening.

Vanessa picked up the phone. "Oh, hey, Jim. I missed your call Sunday."

"I'm so sorry. My Aunt had a bad bout of depression. I took her out on the town to lift her spirits. We didn't get back till late." He sighed. "I sure do miss you."

Torn, Vanessa didn't know how to respond. Her heart yearned for a relationship, but Jim was halfway across the country. She'd had one evening of dinner and conversation with him. She'd painted a picture in her mind of how it could be with Jim. Stability, partners, lovers, and friends were all a part of the landscape she'd envisioned. But the longer Jim was absent from her life, the more he faded from her vision, being replaced by another.

Yes, Jim was halfway across the country. And who knew when he would return.

"I understand," she finally said. "How is she now? Is she feeling better? It must be so very hard for her."

"She's a little better. The whole thing is, I have to find her an apartment. She has to give the house up. She can't maintain it by herself, she's having a bad time with that." Jim sighed again. "Look, I have no idea when I'm going to be done here and it's driving me crazy that I can't see you. Is there any way I can get you to come out here?"

"Oh, no Jim. I have a job. I couldn't afford to—"

"Oh, I'll pay for everything."

"Jim, I'm sorry. I can't afford time off from work. I have my home, my puppy, I can't pick up and leave."

"I know. It was a pipe dream. I feel like the train is taking off and I'm not on it. I can feel you slipping through my fingers. I know it's none of my business, but have you met someone?"

Vanessa's heart stopped. Had she? She sat in silence for a moment, letting the silence spin out like tendrils of a spider's silk.

"Umm. I've kept my options open, Jim. I wouldn't say I've met someone, per say, but . . ." Her voice trailed off.

"Well, God plays his hand. Just know this, pretty lady, I'll never give up. We belong together. I'll never push you. But one day . . . one day will come and it'll be our turn. You take care, now. You know my number; I'll wait for you to call me." He hung up the phone.

She knew she should probably be upset. But things had been set in motion by her mind and her body.

"What has that man done to me?"

* * *

The next few days after work were filled with flirtatious glances between herself and Lamar. As though voicing her possible interest had actually ignited it.

She pulled into her drive on Thursday to discover a clean-cut Adam. His hair was styled nicely, his work clothes were worn, but they were clean aside from the dirt of his labors of the day.

Vanessa waved and walked toward the house. "Hi, Adam. Good to see you. Lamar said you were on another job."

"Yes, ma'am. I finished it up yesterday and Lamar said he could use my help." He shrugged with a smile. "So, here I am."

"I couldn't be happier for you, Adam. I'm very proud of you." She gave him a quick hug and went into the house smiling at his embarrassed blush.

"Dinner for the girl's night tonight?" Lamar met her coming in the back door. The rose garden fence had nearly been completed with Adam's help for the day.

"Yep. Every Thursday." She looked out the back door. "It's really looking good out there."

"With Adam's help, I can probably have it completed by tomorrow. Then I guess you'll have to tell me what the next project is."

"Well, I was thinking it's about time to redo the floor in the bedroom. There're creaking boards and a dip by my bureau." Vanessa thought a moment. "And the plumbing in the private bath needs something. I'm not sure what. You could probably figure it out."

"Mmm. The bedroom. Now that's a project I can take on." Lamar went to put his arms around her, sending waves of heat in all the right places. He stopped short. Gravel crunched in the driveway.

"Sounds like your friend's come early for dinner again. We'll get the tools picked up and head on out." He went back out the garden door.

Vanessa shook her head. "Does she never stop?"

She let Shiela in the front door. "You pour the wine. I've got to change out of my uniform."

"Talk about slingin' orders." Sheila sashayed into the kitchen.

"Talk about showing up carly. Again."

"I had nothing else to do, so I figured I'd mosey on over and get a look at that—Oh, hey there." Sheila put her hand on the hip she'd thrust out.

"Hey, yourself." Lamar sounded aloof.

Vanessa did an about face and went back into the kitchen. "Lamar was just leaving for the day." She turned to him. "Got everything?"

"For now. See you later." He gave both ladies his two fingered salute.

"Don't leave on my account, Sugar." Sheila flashed an open-mouthed smile and winked.

Lamar chuckled on his way out the door.

Sheila's behavior turned normal for the rest of the evening. Vanessa finally relaxed enough to enjoy her company, accepting the fact that her friend was a vixen.

*   *   *

Vanessa surfaced slowly from her deep sleep. *Is that knocking?* Alarmed, she jolted upright in bed and glanced at the clock. "It's one o'clock in the morning."

She swung her feet out of bed and grabbed her robe. "All right, all right. I'm coming," she said to the persistent knocking.

She figured it was Sheila wanting to crash on her couch. *She and Steven must have had an argument.*

She yanked the door open about to tell her friend, thanks a lot for the early morning inconvenience.

The words stuck in her throat.

Lamar stood there with his lopsided grin. He leaned with his hand on the jamb of the door.

"I couldn't sleep. I figured maybe I could start on that project we spoke of earlier." He slipped his hands inside her robe. "You game, pretty lady?"

Her breath caught in her throat when he pulled her into him.

They stumbled over each other furiously fondling their way into the bedroom.

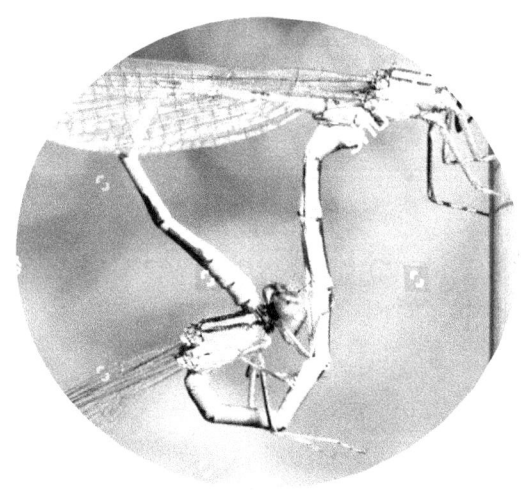

Dragonflies are connected to **Freya,** the goddess of love, war, and fertility, in Norse mythology. Some think they are her symbol because mating dragonflies form the shape of a heart.

19

*F*loating through her work day, exhausted, yet exhilarated, Vanessa had a smile on her face.

She went in to room 416 to treat her favorite patient.

"Well, now. There's the dragonfly I haven't seen in . . ." Mr. Smith put his hand to his chin in consideration. "Let me think, I'd say never. You're sparkling, girl. You got a beau?"

Vanessa chuckled, thought a minute, then said, "Maybe I do."

They both laughed.

"Well, let's hope this one turns out swell for you." He patted her hand.

"Let's hope so." She mixed his breathing solution.

"Ya know, I can't for the life of me figure out why, with you being so mean and torturing me all the time, but I've got a soft spot in my heart for you, girl." The old man chuckled. It turned into a coughing fit.

Alarmed, Vanessa went to her knees beside him to calm and comfort him. "There now. Don't you go getting sick on me again."

His coughing subsided; Mr. Smith nodded his okay for her to administer the treatment. "Just take it easy on me today, dragonfly. I'm not up to much today."

Vanessa smiled, and turned to hook up the hoses. She did her best to hide the tears in her eyes from him. Her heart ached, the happiness welling in her all day momentarily forgotten. Mr. Smith's episodes were becoming so much more frequent. It frightened her.

*   *   *

Vanessa hummed under her breath. She was cooking dinner; pork chops and mashed potatoes with gravy tonight.

Lamar was coming for dinner again. The past few months he'd joined her for dinner. If Adam was working with him for the day, Lamar took him home and returned. If Adam wasn't there that day, Lamar would just stay. Their occasional trysts in the afternoon left them both sated but tired. Those were usually take-out or delivery nights for meals.

She turned the chops over in the pan and felt arms slip around her waist.

She let out a little involuntary scream. "Are you trying to give me a heart attack?" She admonished. "I didn't even hear you pull up. Where'd you park?"

"Right outside in the drive, like always."

"I must have been in my own little world." She turned, spatula in hand, melding their bodies together.

Heat rose in all the right places too quickly. "Oops. Too early for that. Let me get dinner cooked." She stepped away. "Why don't you set the table."

"Only if I can pour the wine, too." He kissed her neck sending shivers down her spine.

All through dinner, Vanessa surreptitiously watched him, gauged his mannerisms, and listened to his easy chatter. *He's rough around the edges, but that can be cleaned up.* Sometimes she found his faults endearing; the terrible grammar he used; as though he hadn't been educated, the ear that stuck out, as big as a batwing. They both stuck out, but the left one protruded twice as much as the right.

She was falling in love with the man. He was gentle, kind, considerate; and the sex was incredible. For the first time in a very long time, she felt like a whole woman.

Do I dare hope? Is this my man across the table sharing the load of life with me?

"Say," Lamar said with a mouthful.

"I think its time you met my friend Jake. I did some work for him, way back. His place is impressive. I think you should see it. I want a place like it one day. He's got horses an' a sprawlin' spread." Lamar nodded, putting a bite the size of half the chop in his mouth.

"Yeah, you need to meet him and see his place." His cheek bulged and grease ran down the side of his mouth.

She shook her head and couldn't help but laugh.

"What?" He finally swallowed.

"Good Lord, Lamar. Can't you eat a little slower? Or at least not talk with your mouth full?"

"The food's good, woman." He half stood, reached across the table, and caressed her breast. "It's *all* good." He winked and sat back down to finish his dinner.

*　　*　　*

Jake Hightower's home was quite a ways in the country. Cruising down the road in Vanessa's car, Lamar driving, he told her about his longtime friend.

"Jake and I've been friends for over thirty years. He's been there for me when I needed him, and I've been there for him; more than once."

Vanessa watched the homes sail by out her window. Some had barns, some had pastures with cattle. *It's so lovely out here.*

Lamar continued, "Anyway, like I said, he got this big spread, and he's willed it all to me." He glanced at her with his lopsided grin.

Vanessa didn't know how to respond to this information. It sounded as if he was bragging, but there was a note of sarcastic humor to it. His eyes appeared to bulge so much more than usual. She'd heard that tone, and seen that look before; it always made her uncomfortable. But it was information or a discussion of such small importance, she never paid much attention. This information, however, seemed to be of great importance. An inheritance? Unless of course, Lamar's idea of a big spread was much different than hers.

She finally found her voice. "To you?"

"Oh, yeah, he and his brother don't get along, and since there's nobody else." He pointed his thumb to his chest. "It's me."

They turned off the road onto a long drive. It curved along a finely trimmed pasture where horses grazed. She saw the huge stable in the distance with a sprawling three story homestead.

"It's beautiful." Vanessa's voice was filled with awe.

"Yep." Lamar parked, got out of the car, and walked to the porch steps. Vanessa followed.

An extremely tall man with a cowboy hat and boots sat in a rocker. He tipped his hat with a finger and nodded to Vanessa with a smile. "Ma'am."

"Jake, I want you to meet my friend, Vanessa Graham. Vanessa, this is my longtime friend Jake Hightower."

"Pleased to meet you, Mr. Hightower." Vanessa smiled.

"Pleasure's all mine, ma'am." He looked at Lamar. "I wasn't expecting company, but I guess I could scare up some sweet tea. We could enjoy it out here on the porch for a spell."

Jake got up and went through the screen door.

Vanessa looked at Lamar, embarrassed. "You didn't call ahead?" she whispered fiercely.

"Never do. Go on. Get up the steps. Plant it in a rocker. You'll be fine."

Dragonflies help us by controlling pest insects, such as mosquitoes and biting flies. A single dragonfly can eat between 30 and hundreds of mosquitoes per day.

20

"So, you really like this guy?" Sheila raised her eyebrow, sipping from her wine glass.

"Yeah. I really think I do," Vanessa answered her friend.

They were sitting in Vanessa's rose garden after their girls' night out dinner. The evening sun was an orange glow over her neighbors' trees.

"I mean, he has his quirks, but he's a good man. He's gentle, kind, and considerate," Vanessa explained.

"Quirks like what?" Sheila sat up straighter in her chair.

"Well, he uses terrible English, you know, he talks like an uneducated hick." She giggled. "But it's kind of endearing."

"The only thing I find endearing is that body. Can he really use that package of his?" Sheila grinned with a spark in her eyes.

Vanessa shook her head. "I'm not going there. I know what that spark in your eyes mean. Hands off, girlfriend. I think he might be the partner I'm looking for. There's a lot more to a relationship than sex. I need a companion, somebody who'll help me through good times and bad." Vanessa considered her next words. "And for the most part, I think Lamar fits that bill right now."

"Well, best to ya, girlfriend." Sheila raised her glass in a toast.

Vanessa raised her glass in turn. I met a longtime friend of his last weekend. Jake's a nice guy; a gentleman. So, he must see something in Lamar. It's what really pushed me to a greater level of trust. Ya know, that he may turn out to be what I've needed all these years.

Vanessa got up and refilled their glasses. "I thought Kevin, my ex, was it. I told you about him, from about six years ago? The sex was great, he helped pay the bills—but then he went and started cheating. I can't abide that."

Sheila flapped her hand. "Don't dwell on the negative. You may have somethin' good going on here, so don't think on the bad stuff."

*   *   *

Vanessa looked forward to coming home every day. She usually planned her evening meal on the way home, stopped at the grocery store when she needed. She was grateful Robert no longer worked there; she hated confrontation.

She pulled into her drive to find Lamar still there working. He was alone. She couldn't help but be excited about the possibility of a little bedroom action before dinner.

Vanessa got out of the car. She walked over to where Lamar was repairing the outside sill on her window, unaware of the little strut she had put in her step.

"Hey. How's it going?" she asked.

"Ah, hell." He threw down the hammer with which he was prying a board loose.

"What's the matter?" Her heart fell a little.

"Well, for starters; your damn meddling cost me my helper, it's hot as hell out here, and this damn board just won't let loose." He wiped sweet off his forehead with his sleeve.

My meddling? Vanessa's face dropped its smile. Hurt entered her eyes.

He looked at her face and his crumbled. "I'm sorry, baby. I don't mean to take it out on you. It's a fine thing you got Adam on the right track, and I'm happy for him."

Startled at his change in demeanor, Vanessa said, "Is Adam not coming back? I don't understand."

Lamar chuckled and sighed. He shook his head. "Nah, he ain't comin' back. He got himself so cleaned up and conscientious, somebody snatched him up and hired him. And at a rate I sure as hell couldn't afford."

"I'm sorry, Lamar. Come inside and cool off. I'll get you a cold beer." She put her arm around his shoulder and led him inside.

They sat at the kitchen table. She had poured herself a wine while he gulped down the beer in three swallows.

He pointed to her wineglass. "Mind if I have one of those?"

"Of course. It's too hot for you to work anymore today, I guess, so just relax." She handed him his drink.

Lamar sighed heavily. "Thanks. I'm sorry about earlier. I'm havin' a bitch of a time. My mom's naggin' at me. 'Why ain't you with Sally no more, I never see the kids, you need to fix this and do that, where are you every night?' She's worse than my last marriage." He drank half his wine.

"I know you've probably noticed my work has fallen off a bit. I'm just so damn preoccupied with Mom spewing her venom every night, every morning. She's trying to make me feel guilty, and it's working. I just don't know what to do, baby."

"I thought things were going okay with your mom."

"They were at first. The first few months was okay. She'd do my laundry for me, cook dinner once in a while. But hell, the last six months or so have been a nightmare. From her wanting me to do *her* laundry, cook *her* dinner, to why can't I bring more money home, what I'm bringing isn't enough." He shook his head. "I give her what I got. I gotta put some toward Sally and the kids."

Vanessa looked at the broken man before her.

Yes, at this point, I suppose he is my man. My broken man.

Her heart went out to him. He'd given her hope of a future for almost a year now. He'd made her feel like a woman.

She looked around at her kitchen where he'd repaired her cupboards. She thought of the beautiful flooring in her living room, the mended fence in her rose garden.

He'd helped her love her home again.

"Tell ya what," she hesitated, screwing up her courage. "You're already here every day. You spend the night and eat dinner with me more often than not."

He looked at her with wariness "What are you sayin'?"

Does he think I'm going to demand something from him like his ex-wife? Like his mother?

"What I'm saying is, why don't you just move in here? With me." She smiled. "You're here most of the time anyway. We share just about everything already. It wouldn't be that big of a change."

Lamar jumped up and hugged her. "Oh, babe, you're the greatest. You mean it?"

She laughed. "Yes, I mean it." She held up her finger. "I am going to need a little help. There're the utilities, the food, the wine. I'm going to need help with money for that."

"Oh, hey. No problem. Whatever you need, babe. Whatever you need."

He pulled his shirt off and eyed her closely. "How about I take a shower to clean up? Then I'm ready for a little action before dinner."

He unzipped his jeans and pulled them down, showing her just how ready he was.

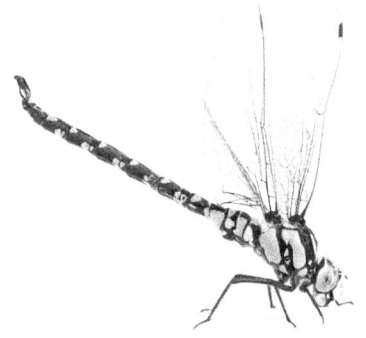

The most common belief related to dragonflies is that they tie to the spiritual world. It's believed they are signs of a loved one, or a guardian angel.

21

*L*amar came in carrying two duffle bags. He dropped them inside her closet on the floor, and shoved them with his foot to the back.

"Is that it?" Vanessa wasn't sure what she was expecting, but it seemed that duffel bags were so transient.

"Got three boxes in the truck. I don't need what's in them much." He pointed to the ceiling. "Attic okay?"

"Sure, you can put them there. Just make sure the entrance is clear. You know, push them over to the side?"

He'd been up in the attic for almost an hour. *What's he doing up there?*

She called up the extended ladder, "Need some help?"

"Nah. Almost done. Just making sure everything's okay." She heard him grunt. "Be down in a jiff."

Minutes later, he came down the ladder. "And don't you worry about dinner tonight." He walked out the front door.

Vanessa stood with her mouth open, then chuckled. "I was just going to ask you what you wanted," she shouted out the door.

Lamar came back in holding a bucket of chicken with his huge crooked grin showing all his teeth.

"Dinnah is served." He bowed.

They both burst out laughing. Vanessa went to take the bucket. He grabbed her and hugged her to him ferociously. The bucket fell to the floor.

"It's got a lid on it," he growled into her neck. "I don't."

They made it to the chicken an hour later, ravenous. Lamar cleaned up the trash and put the leftovers in the fridge.

"Okay, I know you have work tomorrow, but you must come with me. I'll get you back in time to get enough rest." He grabbed her hand and led her to the front door.

"Where are we going?" she protested.

"Never you mind, Missy?"

They took a roundabout way to get across town. Lamar used back roads going through streets lined with oaks, passing houses with azaleas in full bloom. The wind gusted on their faces through the open windows.

Eventually they came back into the town proper and Lamar pulled into Vanessa's favorite ice cream parlor.

Vanessa's heart melted when she saw the look on his face. It was a little boy's, 'Did I do good?' look.

She couldn't get over how sweet his gesture was. This was where she took her boys, her grandbabies, for a treat.

With tears in her eyes, she smiled at him. She pulled his head close and kissed his forehead.

"You're a wonder," she said. And she meant it. This had been the best day she could remember.

*   *   *

Floating through the days at work once more, Vanessa was able to make everyone laugh. Her joy was contagious.

Sheila came up to her after work. "So, tomorrow's Thursday. How's our girls' night out gonna work with this new living arrangement of yours?"

Vanessa stopped. "Oh!"

"Yeah, Oh. Is Lamar going to be joining us for dinner and drinks in your garden?"

"I didn't even think of it. I mean it never crossed my mind." Vanessa giggled.

"I know. What with you havin' so much and all." Sheila scoffed, raising one eyebrow.
"Oh, come on, girl. You've never once asked me over for a girls' night out." Vanessa winked. "You have a life at home, you wouldn't begrudge *me having one too, would you?*"

"I'll just miss my girl." She hugged her. "Tell ya what; why don't we have one last girls' night. I'll tell Lamar to make himself scarce and we'll have us a good ole time."

"Sounds like a plan. See you tomorrow at work." Sheila walked to her car.

On the way home, Vanessa contemplated whether she'd hurt her friend's feelings. She loved Sheila; cherished their relationship. But what she had with Lamar was important, too. She deserved a good life.

* * *

"So, one last blow out for the girls tonight." Lamar said a little too sarcastically for Vanessa's taste.

"Hey, I can't just throw her to the wind. This has been our ritual for years. Sheila's my girl," Vanessa countered defensively.

"And I'm your guy." He pointed to his chest. "I may not be able to buy you expensive tote bags, or anything fancy, but I'm here, baby." He grabbed her around the waist then caressed her backside.

"That's why this is the farewell dinner. The last girls' night for quite some time." She took his hands from her bottom, and kissed his cheek to soften the rebuff.

"Quite some time?" Lamar questioned.

"Well, maybe we'll do a couples' night, you know, the four of us? Anyway, you need to make yourself scarce so I can get on with making these tacos." She shooed him out of the kitchen.

"All right. I guess I'll go visit my mom." He walked back and kissed her cheek.

*   *   *

"Tacos! Just the way we started this," Sheila said when she walked through the door.

"Fitting, no?" Vanessa held a wine glass out to her, raising her own in salute.

"To us."

"To our friendship; partners in crime," Sheila toasted.

Their evening was filled with laughter. Hashing up old trials and tribulations the both of them had faced together: Sheila almost getting caught in the hotel room by Steven until Vanessa came up with a cover story for her, Vanessa almost getting scammed by the internet jerk that tried to convince her he needed $5,000.

Vanessa watched her friend lovingly. In the middle of a laugh that came from her belly, Sheila sighed deeply and stared at the kitchen door. Her eyes looking hungry; the same look in the eyes of the guy Sheila tried to hook her up with in Sparks.

Vanessa's laugh quieted, then died. She turned to see what her friend was looking at so rapturously.

"Hey, Mom had to go to bed. She kicked me out." Lamar stood in the doorway with his own glass of wine.

"Oh, hey. I think our girls' night is about done." Vanessa turned to Sheila. "What do you say, Sheila?"

Sheila put her wine glass down on the table and stood. "I can take a hint. No worries." Her eyes never left Lamar standing in the doorway. "There'll be other times."

Vanessa scrambled up to walk her out the door.

"What was that all about?" Lamar asked when she came back into the kitchen.

"Oh, nothing. I think she's just protective of our friendship. I'm turning in." She rinsed her glass and left.

Vanessa went to bed wondering if what she'd told Lamar was the truth. She didn't care for the hungry look in her friend's eyes when she looked at Lamar; *her man.*

22

Vanessa stood looking at Mr. Smith and his wife. Her heart was torn in two; breaking on one half, exuberantly happy on the other.

"I'm going to miss my main trouble maker," she said.

"And I'll miss my torturer-in-chief, dragon-fly." Mr. Smith chuckled. Amazingly it didn't turn into a coughing fit.

He was well enough to go home. A therapist would home visit twice a week for his treatments.

Vanessa reached down and hugged her favorite patient.

"You take care of that man of yours, missy." Mr. Smith winked at her.

"And make sure he takes care of you." He shook his finger in the air.

They all laughed.

Vanessa gave Mrs. Smith a quick hug. The patient care technician wheeled the chair through the door, taking Mr. Smith out of her life.

Vanessa pulled up in her drive, noticing her hedges needed trimming, the grass needed cutting.

The past few months, Lamar hadn't been getting much done. At first, he'd blamed it on not having Adam to help. *Well, he doesn't need Adam's help to trim the hedges and mow the lawn.*

She went in the house intending to mention it, but stopped short when she walked into the living room.

A beautiful vase of flowers stood on the coffee table. Before she thought, she blurted out, "Where'd you get the money to buy those?"

Lamar stood from lounging on the couch. "What kind of question is that? I get my lady some flowers to show my love and you come in and ask where I got the money?" His eyes had started to bug out.

She knew that wasn't a good sign, but she couldn't help herself. "Well, they're beautiful, Lamar. But I had to pay the electric bill late this month. Things have gotten tight lately. I've got the only income right now. We just need to tighten up a little." She thought a moment. "And maybe you—"

Lamar slammed the magazine he'd been reading down on the coffee table. "Maybe I could do what?" Spittle flew from his angry mouth.

Vanessa could feel the heat rising in her face. "Well, maybe you could find a job. I mean other than here. I can't support food, water, electricity, and booze for two people and then pay you too."

"Well, isn't that just swell. You'd ruin anybody's day; I go out and do something nice for you and you just trash it. Trash *it* and trash *me*."

"Lamar, I—"

"Never mind." He grabbed his keys and headed to the door. "I'll save you some money on food. I'm going to Mom's for dinner. Don't wait up for me."

Vanessa stood with tears flowing down her cheeks. Her happiness for Mr. Smith's recovery, and her joy for life itself, was sucked into a black hole of confusion.

*   *   *

Lamar stayed gone for three days. Vanessa missed him. She vacillated between being mad at him, and wondering if she hadn't been too hard on him.

On the fourth day, Vanessa pulled into her drive to see Lamar's pickup sitting there. The lawn had been mowed.

Relief with trepidation filled her. She went into the house. It smelled delicious.

Lamar poked his head out of the kitchen door. "I figured I couldn't mess up hamburgers." He smiled his brightest smile. "Ya hungry?"

Vanessa couldn't help but smile back. "Um, yeah, I guess."

"Well, change your clothes and I'll get your wine. We're having burgers, lady." He went back to the stove.

Confused, walking on eggshells, Vanessa complied.

She sat at the table in front of the wine he'd poured for her. He set the plated burger on the table.

Lamar knelt beside her chair. "I'm so sorry, baby. I was in a funk and overreacted when you called me on it." He took her hand and kissed it. "Can you forgive my temper tantrum?"

He stood and went to sit at his own plate. "Oh, And I got a job." He took a bite of burger; mayonnaise dripped down the crease of his mouth. "A lady needs her back deck redone. That means tearing it down, building it, staining it, everything. It's a good job."

Vanessa relaxed. "That sounds great, hon. You like that kind of work." She began eating her own meal.

"Yeah, she knows lots of people. I'll probably get some recommendations, turn 'em into more jobs."

"The lawn looks wonderful." She sipped her wine.

They eased their way into their normal comfortability.

"Say. You know what I was thinking? I'm not too shabby at burgers. Why don't we have a cookout? You know, invite some people we know? You could invite that friend of yours and her husband. I'll ask Mom." He thought a minute. "I could ask Adam—word has it, he has a girl." Lamar chuckled. "You really did clean him up."

"That sounds nice, Lamar. I think I'd like that. Sheila and Steven could bring their kids and I'll see if my grandkids could come." She was getting more excited the more they planned together, like a family. "I can make potato salad." She giggled.

"I love your potato salad. But you know what I'm hungry for right now?" He came around the table, lifted her and carried her to the bedroom.

"I've missed you, baby," he growled in her ear.

She'd missed him, too.

23

Vanessa sat beside Lamar in church. The cookout had been two weeks ago and everyone had had a blast. Sheila and Steven brought their kids, hotdogs, and potato chips. Lamar's mom had come, but Vanessa felt a little snubbed. When Vanessa would walk over to talk to her, it seemed as though Mrs. Wilson would find something or someone of interest across the yard. She'd say "Oh, excuse me dear, I just—" her voice would trail off as she walked away.

Adam's girlfriend was sweet and charming. He appeared to be a very happy young man.

The party ended after Steven won at horseshoes. He mostly ignored the flirtations Sheila sent Lamar's way. Vanessa didn't miss them, though. Nor did she miss the way Sheila constantly sought him out with that look in her eyes.

Vanessa chalked it up to her friend's promiscuity. Sheila would never do anything to hurt her, never. They were closer than sisters.

The reverend raised his voice along with his arms, preaching the gospel. Her attention came back to the present.

When the sermon ended, everyone shuffled out the front door. A young woman bumped into Lamar, seemingly by accident.

Her eyes widened in recognition of him. "Oh, Lamar." She smiled sheepishly. "How are you?" She gave a sideways glance at Vanessa.

Lamar did his two-finger salute and nodded once. "Millie."

He steered Vanessa out the door and to the car.

"Who was that?" she asked, closing her passenger door.

"Who?" Lamar started the car. He didn't look at her.

"The girl that bumped into you. You called her Millie."

"Oh, Millie? She used to go to my old church. You know, where Sally and I went?" He glanced at her quickly. "She must have changed churches too." His face darkened like it had before slamming the magazine on the table and storming out.

Then, Lamar brightened. "Hey. Want to get the grandkids and go out for ice cream?"

Relieved at his shift in moods, Vanessa smiled wide. "That sounds wonderful. I could use a dose of my babies since they couldn't make it to the cookout."

Knowing her grandkids' laughter and antics would be good medicine for her spirits, she looked forward to the rest of the day.

*   *   *

Vanessa made Lamar breakfast before sending him off to work. She had agreed to have lunch with Sheila that afternoon since they had the same days off.

Vanessa walked into the restaurant. Sheila was already seated with two glasses of wine on the table.

"I only ordered your wine. I didn't know what you'd want for lunch, but you know what I'm having." Sheila got up and hugged her hello.

Vanessa had grilled chicken salad while Sheila ate her tacos. Their conversation was light, filled with Sheila's latest extra-marital escapades.

"And speaking of hot men, how's your love life?" she asked Vanessa.

Vanessa put her fork down. "My *life* is great. Including home, work, relationship . . . and love, if you insist."

"Well, good. But listen; I'd be careful of that one if I were you," she warned.

"What do you mean, be careful of that one?'" Vanessa asked.

"Well, I've heard things," Sheila hedged.

Vanessa's eyebrows shot up. "Heard things? From whom?"

"Well, Let's just say I asked around." Sheila took a bite of her taco and chewed lazily, eyeing Vanessa the whole while.

"First of all," she continued, "he's known as a womanizer. Which is surprising, because he comes from a good family."

"That's just nonsense gossip. I can't believe you're even bringing this to me." Vanessa sounded disgusted; she was.

"No, no. Not nonsense gossip. He was caught having an affair with another church member." Sheila nodded, happy to prove her point.

"Look, I know you're trying to protect me, but I know all about the affair. He told me about it. He regretted it, it pretty much ruined his marriage, but he's moved on now." Vanessa tried not to sound defensive, but she couldn't help but think about Millie.

She dismissed the thought immediately. "Definitely moved on. Neither one of us are left wanting in that department." Vanessa couldn't help but let out a little giggle.

On the way home Vanessa's mind was filled with loving thoughts of her best friend, she knew Sheila truly cared for her, always trying to protect her from hurt or harm in anyway. She counted herself more than fortunate to have someone who cared as much as Sheila in her life.

*   *   *

When she walked in the door, she found Lamar was already home. "Hey, where's your truck?"

She saw a single red rose on the coffee table with papers tied to the stem.

"It's at the shop. Needs a tune-up. And since I've been steady working and got another job on the line after this one, I figured we could use a break." He pointed to the rose. "Go ahead, pick it up."

Vanessa went over and untied the paperwork from the rose. It was a receipt for two nights in a cabin in the mountains. The lodge had swimming, tennis, two restaurants, and a guided tour of some trails.

She gasped. She'd always wanted to take a trip like this.

"I know you have seniority at work, and I know your boss. You can't say no." He hugged her.

24

V anessa and Lamar played word games on the four-hour drive to their mountain get away.

They went on walks through the woods, they visited both restaurants, but most of their time was spent in the cabin. Invigorated by the change in scenery and fresh mountain air, they both applied new energy to their lovemaking. There wasn't a room or spot in the cabin they hadn't christened by the end of their long weekend.

Vanessa fell more deeply in love with every passing day. Lamar made her laugh, he caressed her womanly soul.

On their last night, Vanessa and Lamar lay in front of the fireplace with wine. Vanessa watched the flames flicker with red tipped fingers of fire.

"Hey, you," Lamar said in a soft voice beside her.

She turned to him and looked into his eyes. They were tender, reflecting the fire. He grinned at her, no smile to expose his teeth. *He looks beautiful in this light.* "Hmm?" she muttered the question.

"I was thinking about something." He turned his gaze away and sipped his wine.

"Thinking about what?" she asked.

"Thinking about us. You know, maybe making this more permanent." He leaned over and kissed her, turning passionate, not giving her a chance to think or respond to what he'd just suggested.

*   *   *

Vanessa startled awake. Children's laughter carried through the opened windows. She and Lamar were still on the blanket, the fire had burned out. "Oh my gosh. We better get going, what time is it?" She threw on her nightgown and scurried to the kitchen. "9:30! Lamar it's almost time to check out." She ran to him and shook his shoulder.

"Whaa?" He struggled to sit up.

"It's almost checkout time. We've got to get everything together." She went to the bedroom and frantically packed their clothes.

They grabbed coffees to go and headed home. There were no word games on the way home. Vanessa stared at the scenery. Trees and pastures that looked like the color green was named after. Red tailed hawks flying high overhead, catching the air currents and sailing lazily in patterns.

Vanessa thought of Lamar's, "Maybe making this more permanent." She hadn't felt so good since she'd met and fell in love with her ex. *Look how that turned out. I don't want any repeats.*

As though reading her thoughts, Lamar asked, "So, have you thought about what we talked about last night?"

She sighed and looked at him. They were getting along so well as they were. She didn't want to ruin that.

"I just need more time, Lamar. We're doing so well. Let's just take things slow for now."

"I can do that." He gave her his two-finger salute and turned back to look at the road.

She saw the muscles of his jaw working.

*   *   *

Two weeks later, Vanessa came home to find Lamar already there. She walked in the house to find him laying on the couch with a beer watching a soap opera on the television.

"Hey, you home already?" She headed toward the bedroom.

"Yes. I'm home already." His voice was high pitched, as though he were mocking her.

She stopped and looked at him.

"I finished the job, okay?" He swigged his beer.

"Well, that's good, right?" She was confused as to his attitude.

"It would be if the woman she recommended me to was ready to have her work done. But she's not."

"Well, maybe she'll be ready soon, or you'll find something else," she consoled him.

"I don't know when she'll be ready, if ever. And yeah, I'll find something else. I just don't need you crawling my ass about it." He got up, went into the kitchen, and got another beer.

For the next month, Vanessa walked on eggshells. Bills had piled up and the stress of getting bad credit leeched her energy.

She'd asked Lamar once if there were any prospects for a job and he exploded, punching a hole in the bathroom wall.

At lunch with Sheila, she poured her heart out. Fighting back tears she complained, "He's in bed when I leave in the morning and on the couch when I get home."

"Well, honey, it sounds like you need to get rid of that man. What good is he?" Sheila asked.

"Things can be so good with us. I think he's in a slump." Vanessa pushed the food around on her plate.

"He needs to unslump himself. Unless you don't mind payin' for stud service." Sheila chuckled not unsympathetically.

"Oh, I don't even have that. He hasn't touched me in weeks. I think I'm going to take on overtime. As much as I can get. That'll take the pressure off." Vanessa attempted to smile.

"Hang in there, girlfriend. If I were you, I'd kick him to the curb, but you're kindhearted and way too forgiving, if you ask me."

*   *   *

On her third month of working sixty to seventy hour weeks, Vanessa drug herself out of bed. She'd been chalking up her exhaustion to so much work, but decided it was time for a check-up with her doctor.

She'd arranged to work the late shift, and forget about the overtime for one day. She slept in.

"Why aren't you at work?" Lamar asked her when he got up.

Sleepily, she opened her eyes. "Huh? What?"

"I said why aren't you at work?"

"Doctor's appointment. I'm going in late." She explained.

"Doctor's appointment. Great. That's just what we need, you getting sick." He slammed the bedroom door when he went out.

Vanessa drug herself through the next two weeks, then she got a call from her doctor.

The news wasn't good. It was breast cancer. In shock, Vanessa hung up the phone, not sure what to do.

Lamar was laying on the couch. He'd overheard the portion of her conversation with the doctor where she'd made the appointment to go back in for her consultation.

"Another doctor's appointment? I hope you don't expect me to help pay for all this," he snarled.

Rage bloomed in her chest. Before she thought better of it, she said, "You don't help for anything else. Why would I expect you to help with this?"

"Don't you worry. I've got a job coming up, you don't have to rub it in my face." He got up and stormed out.

She heard his truck tearing down her drive. *What am I going to do? How am I going to tell him?*

Vanessa burst into tears.

The males of some dragonfly species are highly territorial. Competitors will fight viciously over prime egg-laying sites in order to attract the most females.

25

*L*ook, you're my best friend, I expect support. Not this worry and doubt. The doctor gave me every indication that I'm going to come through this just fine." The restaurant was bustling with the packed lunch crowd.

"I know, but I can't help but worry." Sheila's face was tight with concern.

"I'm supposed to keep a positive attitude, Sheila. Worry isn't positive. I'm not telling Lamar until I absolutely have to, so I really need you to be there for me when I get weak and doubtful. You're supposed to by my anchor." She grabbed her friend's hand. "I need you."

"I got it." Sheila sipped her wine. "You just took me by surprise, that's all. I got your back, Nessa. I promise."

They finished up lunch on a lighter note. Talking of Sheila's sexual exploits and the antics of her boys.

When Vanessa got home Lamar was no where to be seen. She took advantage of the privacy to soak in a nice hot bath, relax, and take a nap.

She woke to darkness and an empty house. *I guess I better think about putting something on for dinner. Lamar must be on a job.*

She called his number to see what time to have dinner ready.

No answer.

Vanessa busied herself frying chicken thinking it would be easy to heat up and she could snack on it tomorrow after her two shifts.

She was sitting in her garden with a glass of wine when Lamar sauntered in. She was angry. She'd called him five times over the past four hours. There'd been no answer.

"Where've you been?" A hard edge tinged her voice.

"Working. It's just a one-day job. They'll pay me next week. What's wrong with you?"

"I called you five times. You can't answer your phone and let me know you're alive?"

"I left the phone in the truck." He threw a twenty dollar bill at her. "They gave me money for gas since they can't pay me for the job 'til next week. And for your information, I haven't even looked at my phone. I just wanted to get home." He leaned down and kissed her. "Sorry, I'm just tired."

Vanessa relented. When he worked, he did work hard. "There's chicken. I fried some up with mashed potatoes and green beans."

"Sorry, babe. I already ate. I'm hittin' the sack after a shower." He turned and walked back into the house.

* * *

"Morning, John." Vanessa walked into the records room.

"Honey, you've got to take a break. You look dead on your feet." John got up and hugged her lightly; as though she would break.

"I know, John. The treatments are really taking it out of me. I've lost my appetite."

"You'll get through this, my friend. Have you told Lamar yet?" John sat back down at his computer.

"No." Vanessa sighed. "I'm going to have to soon, though. Eventually he's going to notice I'm not really eating and I'm frequenting the bathroom to get sick much too often."

"Hang in there, girl. I send daily prayers your way." He glanced toward the door.

Susan had walked in with a load of files in her arms. She stopped and looked at Vanessa.

"Don't mention it, Suz. She knows already. Just hug her some energy and send her on her way." John went back to work.

Susan did as he bade, giving Vanessa a warm smile.

Vanessa made her rounds then went down after her break to get her list of patients for the next shift. She looked at her paperwork and her mouth dropped open.

Mr. Smith, room 216.

"Oh, Mr. Smith. What are you doing back here?" She shook her head and hurried to his room.

Vanessa didn't bother with her previous playfulness of peeking in his room. She burst through the door praying he was in decent shape.

He lay there with the oxygen mask fitting over his face. His eyes were closed. Her heart stopped.

She went to his bed and gently held his wrist to check the pulse.

His eyes fluttered open. "Dragonfly." He croaked.

"Mr. Smith. I missed you, but I'd rather miss you than see you back here."

He patted her hand. "I just couldn't stay away from your sunshine." He dropped back off to sleep.

*   *   *

Vanessa pushed the food around on her plate. Lamar had been nice enough to make dinner.

He looked up at her. "What's the matter with you? I made this casserole because I knew you worked four doubles in a row. I was trying to make an effort, but if you're not going to appreciate it . . ."

"I really do appreciate it, Lamar. I just don't have an appetite." She tried to take a bite, then got up and rushed to the bathroom.

When she came back, he'd replaced his empty plate with a beer. He sat there glaring at her.

"Listen, hon, we have to talk. I've just been looking for a way to tell you." She went to the fridge and got some ginger ale.

"Just out with it and let's get it over with." He slugged his beer.

Vanessa took a deep breath to steady herself. "I have breast cancer. The treatments are what's making me so sick. But I'll be done with them soon. And things should start getting back to normal."

"You've been getting treatments behind my back?" He stood up, eyes bulging. "Why would you do that? You let me sit here and talk marriage and shit, and you say nothing?"

Vanessa's head was swimming. She was so exhausted it was hard to think. "I'm trying to stay positive, it's important for my health. I knew you'd be worried; I didn't want to put stress and worry on you." She burst into tears.

"Well, you can save the tears. If it gets bad, or worse than this, I'm not gonna be around to wait on you, hand and foot. I ain't no caretaker."

He threw his empty bottle in the trash and got another. "You should go to bed and get your rest. You even *look* like you need it."

He turned back halfway through the door. "I'm going for a drive. Don't wait up."

The door slammed.

The emptiness that filled her heart was vacuous. She sank into her bed, the pillow enveloped her tired mind, and she finally drifted into blessed nothingness.

To some, seeing a dragonfly may be a message that you are about to make a change in your life.

26

Vanessa felt better after resting for a few days. Her doctor had ordered her to work less. She had to at least quit the overtime; it was interfering in her body's fight.

She tried calling Sheila a couple of times. Stephen informed her that Sheila had gone somewhere for her days off; he didn't know where. She'd needed some alone time away from the kids.

Vanessa was surprised that Sheila hadn't mentioned it to her. She was disappointed she didn't have her friend to confide in. There was good news and bad. Mr. Smith was off continuous oxygen and taking his regular breathing treatments. And Vanessa hadn't heard from Lamar in the three days since she'd told him about her cancer.

On the fourth day of Lamar's absence, Vanessa pulled into her drive to find his truck there. Too tired to fight with him, she went into the house, raised her hand in acknowledgement and said, "Hey."

She went in to change her clothes then went in to the kitchen to heat up some soup. It was the only thing she could keep down.

He followed her and sat at the table with his beer.

"Don't you want to ask me where I've been?" he asked.

"Should I?" she countered.

"Only if you want to know." He smirked at her, and took three gulps of his beer.

"I'm not so sure that I do," she said wearily. "Look, Lamar, I'm tired. I don't want to argue. I want to try to get some of this soup down, and go to bed. I have to work tomorrow and I can't mess it up. I had to quit overtime and I need this job."

"Well, I'm just in time, then." He pulled out a wad of bills and laid them on the table. "I was working. It was a job in Alabama so I couldn't get home every night. I finished there and I've got more lined up here, close to home."

Vanessa was too tired to be relieved. She gave him a weak smile.

Lamar got up and kissed her kerchiefed head. The past few months had claimed her hair. "You're just as beautiful as ever. I'm sorry I stormed out the other day; for the mean things I said. I guess I was just scared. I don't want to lose you, babe." He picked her up, carried her to the bedroom, bathed her and put her in bed.

*   *   *

Lamar was at his mother's. She had a bad cold, and he needed to spend the night with her. Vanessa asked him to make sure he didn't bring anything home to her; her body wouldn't be able to fight it. He'd agreed to stay for a few days to make sure he hadn't caught his mother's cold.

Sheila and Vanessa took the opportunity for a rare girls' night get together. Sheila brought chicken pot pie hoping Vanessa could keep it down.

"You did a decent job of that." Sheila pointed to Vanessa's half eaten pie. Most of the gravy and a few vegetables were gone.

"It actually tasted pretty good." Vanessa smiled back at her friend.

"So, is Lamar treating you right?" Sheila asked.

Vanessa shrugged. "Sometimes. I never know when he's going to fly off the handle and walk out. He's being real nice right now. He's working. That's something in itself." She sipped her ginger ale. "But, like the time I told him I had cancer, he just exploded and walked out. It kills me when he does that; we can be so good together."

"I'm here for ya, kiddo. Let's just get you well. Then we'll figure out what to do with your man." Sheila patted her hand.

"I don't know what I'd do without you, Sheila. You're always there for me. I couldn't live without my best friend."

"Well, just don't ever forget, you can count on me."

*   *   *

Vanessa walked into the records room. John and Susan both stopped what they were doing and looked at her.

"What is it, guys? What's wrong?" Vanessa's stomach knotted into a pit.

Susan walked over to Vanessa and embraced her. "I'm so sorry, Ness. Mr. Smith passed away last night."

Vanessa's body stiffened, going into shock.

John jumped up and went to them, putting his arms around both women. "Breathe, girl," he told Vanessa. "Just breathe. Come on. Let's sit you down and get you some water."

Vanessa took a deep breath, sipped the water John had brought and collapsed into a chair.

"He was my friend," she sobbed. "I loved him. He called me his dragonfly—" her voice hitched. "His dragonfly."

"I know, I know honey," John consoled. "Suz? Are you off duty now? Can you take her home? She can't work like this. I'll call her boss."

Vanessa pulled herself together over the next couple of days. Lamar was not supportive with her grief. But at least he didn't belittle her feelings.

Mr. Smith's funeral was Saturday. Vanessa went home Friday evening after work and started laying her clothes out for the funeral. "Lamar, do you want me to get your dark blue shirt ready for tomorrow?"

"For what?" he called from the couch.

"For Mr. Smith's funeral. You're coming with me, right?"

"For what? I don't know that man. I ain't goin' to no funeral. Forget it."

Vanessa's grief surfaced all over again. She tried to swallow back the tears unsuccessfully.

Lamar got up off the couch and went in to the bedroom. "What are you all upset about? He's just an old man you hardly even knew. What's the big deal?"

Vanessa couldn't speak lest she burst into sobs.

"I had to live through your blubbering for days. I'm sick of this. I'm not going and you shouldn't either. For God's sake." He grabbed his keys off the dresser. "I'll be back when you pull yourself together, damn it."

Slamming doors, the engine revving, spinning gravel, and he was gone.

Vanessa pulled herself together for the funeral the next day. *At least I'll have my best friend by my side. Sheila wouldn't miss this, and I need somebody.*

She walked down the aisle looking left and right at the pews. No Sheila. Everyone was either teary eyed or sobbing when the reverend ended his sermon.

At the gravesite, Vanessa looked around at the people gathered. Still, her friend was absent. *Something must have happened.* She went and hugged Mrs. Smith.

"You're such a sweet dear. He thought so highly of you." Mrs. Smith hugged her back.

"He was one of my favorite people on earth, Mrs. Smith. I'm so sorry for everyone's loss. I'll pray for your heart to heal." Vanessa squeezed the old woman's hand, and walked to her car.

She walked in to her empty home. *Perfect. It's exactly how I feel.*

The Amberwing dragonfly, like all dragonflies, has two sets of wings. If one of them breaks, it can still fly. The ability to carry on no matter the hurt, was the reason for Amberwing's name.

27

Vanessa drug herself to church the day after Mr. Smith's funeral. She sat in the pew alone and scrutinized the congregation. *What am I looking for? Who am I looking for?*

Then she saw her. Millie. One row back across the aisle, the woman sat there staring at Vanessa.

Their eyes met. Millie raised one eyebrow, tilted her head in a slight nod, and smirked.

A cold chill ran down Vanessa's spine. A feverish blush rose to her cheeks. *What was that message? Was she taunting me?*

Vanessa snapped her head forward and grabbed her purse. She waited for a hymn to be sung, then walked out. Her head held high and proud, she never once glanced to either side.

She arrived home. The driveway was empty— no one home but her and Bella, apparently. She was slumped in her car, gathering her wits. *Why did that woman have such an effect on me? And what was that smirk all about? Why was I even thinking about looking around to see who was at church?* She shook her head. "You know why. That day running into Lamar and his strangely reluctant answer as to who she was, wasn't right. That's why."

Vanessa got out of her car, went into the house, hugged Bella, and took her exhausted body back to bed.

That evening she rose to try and get down some soup. Vanessa decided to call Sheila. She hadn't really talked to her best friend since their last girls' night out.

Sheila picked up on the first ring.

"How's it going?" Vanessa tried to put a little cheer in her voice, and failed miserably.

"How is it with you? Are you okay?" The concern in Sheila's voice was palpable.

Vanessa sighed. "Yeah. Just tired. I can't wait for these treatments to be over." She paused. "Say, I was looking for you at the funeral. I missed you."

"Oh, yeah. Well, Steven had something planned with the boys without telling me. He thought more family time would help keep Donnie out of trouble. I'm sure you're the only one that missed me." Sheila chuckled.

"Maybe so. I really needed a friend. Lamar refused to go. Said I shouldn't go either, that Mr. Smith was just an old man I hardly knew; that *he* didn't know at all."

"I know." Sheila sounded disgusted.

Vanessa thought a moment. Sheila's comment struck her strangely. "What do you mean, 'you know'?"

"Oh, It's just the way he is from what you tell me. I mean, I figured that would be something he'd say." Ice cubes rattled. "I'm sorry I wasn't there for you."

"S'okay. Look, I gotta lay back down. I'm exhausted."

"Well, call me if you need anything."

The phone clicked. Sheila'd hung up before Vanessa could say goodbye.

*   *   *

Vanessa's work week was grueling; even though it was only three half days. Lamar was back on Monday. He came home from work with chicken pot pie.

He handed it to her and said, "Here, I thought maybe you could keep some of this down."

"Thanks, maybe I can. Thanks for being sweet." Vanessa began picking through the pie, spooning the gravy and a few vegetables.

"Enjoy it. You need to get better. I can't afford bringing you stuff home every night. Not with you working part-time." He turned to leave the room.

"Well, that may be something we need to talk about, because I may need to quit the part-time for a while. I don't think I can keep it up much longer."

He turned back to her. "I was going to tell you; you need a rich man. And I'm not him. Now? Now! You don't only need a rich man, you need a really rich man. And good luck with that, sweetheart. It takes at least one of two things to land a man, and right now you ain't got either of 'em." He went to the fridge, grabbed a beer, and stalked into the living room.

Vanessa sat there with her mouth open. Tears welled in her eyes.

A second later, he stomped back in; hands on hips. "And I'll tell you another thing. Here I am, catering to your every need, and for what?

"If something happens to my mama, I get everything; it's all willed to me. If something happens to you—I get nothing." He pointed his finger, spittle spraying from his mouth.

"So you tell me why I even care if you eat or not." He stormed back out.

Vanessa heard the television come on to a game show. Her stomach clenched. She rose, tipping over her chair, then ran into her bathroom and vomited into her toilet.

The next day, Vanessa lay in bed; grateful she didn't have work. She heard Lamar talking to someone in the kitchen; only *his* voice—he must have been on the phone.

She heard him laugh. She could only make out a few words. *I know, baby, me too – laughter - . . . too much.*

Vanessa got up, put her robe on and made her way into the kitchen.

"No, not for a couple days. Sorry. Things are a little dicey. But may—"

He'd seen her out of the corner of his eye. "Uh, yeah, maybe one day next week, I'll call ya." He hung up.

"Who was that?" Vanessa steadied herself against the cabinet and reached for a can of soup.

"Nobody. I mean, just a potential job. I told him I'd take a look at it next week." He jumped up from the table. "Here, which one do you want? I'll heat it for you." He kissed her on the forehead.

*   *   *

The next few weeks Vanessa pushed herself harder than she ever had before. Her three half-days became two.

She was grateful. If she hadn't been so exhausted and, in such pain, she'd have been surprised; Lamar was kind, gentle, and loving. He brought her soft foods he thought she'd like and would be able to keep down.

Always on edge—she'd never forget the chicken pot pie incident—she basically waited for the other shoe to drop.

She began to ignore the covert phone calls; always cut short if he heard her moving around the house, or she walked into the room. She was too tired and too insecure for confrontation.

One Sunday, Vanessa decided to stay home from work. She'd made up her mind to give up the part-time work altogether.

She lay in bed dozing when Lamar came in.

"You not going in to work?" he asked.

"I can't," she was almost too tired to respond.

"Well fine, then. I guess you're not going to church either. Well I am. I guess I'll see you when I see you. I'm really sick of this shit." He put on his tie. "Oh, I forgot, you've cornered the market on being sick." He stormed out of the house, slamming every door he came to.

Who were all those phone calls from, or to? Why the mood swings? If she came home early, or didn't go in, he'd find a way to explode over nothing. Where did he go when he disappeared for a day or three? The texting that was abruptly halted.

Vanessa held the account for his phone. *I can pull those records online and find out exactly who he's been communicating with, and what was said.*

She got up and went to the computer.

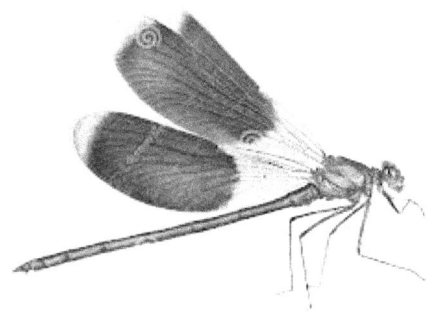

There are more than 5,000 known species of dragonflies, all of which belong to the order Odonata, which means "toothed one" in Greek and refers to the dragonfly's serrated teeth.

28

Vanessa's jaw dropped when she saw the picture. Millie, lips puckered, blouse held open exposing the skimpiest lace bra Vanessa had ever seen. It didn't quite cover the areole.

Another of Millie. A selfie, running her tongue around relaxed lips covered with bright abrasive red.

The texts were somehow worse:

* When you goin' dump that bitch and marry me.

* I love it when you're so hard.

* Ooh baby, make me so hot. How about tomorrow. She has to work.

An endless, shameful, barrage of more of the same. And the phone calls . . . four times a day to or from Millie. And some from Sheila. *Sheila?*

Vanessa's anger boiled over into fear; then self-doubt. What if this was her fault. Lamar had said it took one of two things to land a man. She imagined it was true enough pertaining to keep one, too. She'd lost her hair, and was in so much pain she'd lost her beauty, and she certainly had no energy for sex. Not that he'd really tried. But maybe that was because she was no longer attractive.

But what was she going to do about it? He wasn't perfect, but neither was she. It had been so lonely before. She'd felt lost and alone. He'd made her feel like a woman.

But Sheila? Why?

She called Sheila.

"Why would you call Lamar?" she demanded.

Sheila was silent for a moment; taken aback. "Well, honey . . . uh, I didn't want to disturb you. I was asking how you were. You know? I worry about you."

Vanessa breathed a sigh of relief.

"That bastard's been cheating on me." Vanessa blurted out.

"Wait a minute, Nessa. What are you talking about?" Sheila's voice sounded panicked.

"He cheated on me with that bitch from church, Sheila. I have texts." She sniffed. "And pictures. Pictures of the tramp showing her cleavage—well, it's more than cleavage. She wants him to marry her, Sheila. What am I just a damn doormat to step on and pay for his phone? Then, when I get sick, he just throws me away?" Vanessa's voice crumbled into sobs.

"Oh, Nessa. I'm so sorry. You don't deserve this. I told you that man was no good."

Vanessa composed herself. "I just feel like my whole world has had the plug pulled out. We were so happy. Then I got sick. I couldn't help that. I didn't do it on purpose." A sob escaped her.

Sheila tried to interject something but Vanessa just talked over her in her frenzied grief. "She called me a bitch. When you going to dump that bitch and marry me? That's what she texted. And how far he can stick—oh, never mind. It's disgusting."

Sheila was quiet.

"Is this my fault? I haven't been a good companion lately. I can't do anything. I need almost everything done for me. Sheila, what am I going to do?"

"No, it's not your fault. Sickness and health, richer or poorer, remember. That's what couples are suppose to live by. Maybe he's not committed enough to get married," Sheila consoled.

"Maybe, he can't commit because I never said yes. I wasn't committed. I just liked things the way they were."

"Well, regardless, you still have to confront him about it. See what he has to say for himself," said Sheila.

"I know. I'm just not ready for that yet. I'm so tired, Sheila. I don't have the energy to argue." Vanessa heard the whine in her own voice and wondered if that was one of the things that had driven him away.

"Take your time, Nessa. You're the one in control now. You choose when to address it. Don't let him turn the blame around on you," Sheila warned. "This is not your fault."

Vanessa felt a little better after her talk with Sheila. Anger began to take over her self-doubt. But the fear of being alone never left her heart.

Monday, Vanessa went to her doctor's visit. While she was there, she changed her medical records to read Sheila as the person to notify; the person to make decisions about her health and treatment if she was ever incapable of doing so.

The days went agonizingly slow. Vanessa was better rested now that she wasn't working. But the pain was still there; a constant nagging reminder of her disease, her weakness.

She did her best to maintain their relationship. When he was nice, it wasn't that hard to forget his betrayal. Since his blow out last Sunday, he'd been very decent.

Lamar called before coming home on Friday to ask if she wanted him to bring her something to eat.

"You know, I kind of feel like one of those chicken pot pies. Remember the one you brought me a few weeks ago? That would be nice. Thanks for being so sweet."

"Hey, no problem." He hung up.

In anticipation she got dressed and went to the kitchen. She'd put on her prettiest scarf and tried a little blush and lipstick.

He walked in and dropped the paper bag on the table in front of her. She opened it and took out the pot pie. It smelled heavenly and was still nice and warm.

"You didn't get one for yourself?" She'd hoped they could eat together.

"No, I didn't get one for myself. You're lucky I had enough money to splurge on you." His high pitched, mocking, voice sent her stomach into spasms.

"You think you're the only one I got to spend money on? I gotta give Sally money for the kids. I gotta give my mom money here and there. I'm helping *you* with the bills."

He went to the fridge and got a beer. "You sit here all damn day like some princess. I've had about enough—."

"You think you've had enough?" Vanessa went to her sideboard drawer and pulled out the texts, the pictures, the number of phone calls she'd printed out and threw them at him.

"Is she the reason you're picking a fight? When were you planning on dumping this bitch for that one? You're talking marriage to me while you're all up her ass." She took the pot pie, threw it in the trash and went to the bedroom, closing the door.

It took him five minutes to follow her. Was he compiling his story? His excuses?

He opened the door and walked in, sitting on the edge of the bed. "Hey, babe. It's not what it looks like. Nothing ever happened. We was just texting for the hell of it. Hell, I never asked her to send those pictures. I know it was wrong, I'm sorry. But I swear, I never touched her." He pulled out his phone, punched a few things, then held it out to her. "There. I've blocked her number." He leaned down and kissed her forehead. "It was just a silly stupid game, I swear. I'll never do anything like that again."

Vanessa lay their silently. Running through her mind were thoughts of being alone. She didn't believe him for a second. But what were her options? Loneliness was too empty.

"I'll forget this just once, Lamar. But don't you ever do this to me again. I am not your doormat." She put her hand, palm up, on her forehead.

He rose slowly. "That's the way you wanna be. Alright. But I'll tell you one damn thing. You ever snoop on me again, go through my personal things, you don't even wanna know what'll happen." His voice was low and menacing.

It frightened her, but her anger gave her courage. "I paid for your privilege to betray me. Whether you touched her or not, it was still betrayal."

Lamar pulled his fist back, his eyes bulging, then stopped, turned and walked out.

29

She relived the pulled back fist over and over. Walking on eggshells, lest she reignite his anger, Vanessa got through her days wearily.

Lamar was attentive. He brought her food and took her to doctors' appointments. There were no more covert phone calls, but he was still distant.

Over the months, Vanessa slowly healed. She went back to part time work at the hospital and their relationship started knitting itself back together.

Lamar was on a job—lately they were few and far between. Vanessa was resting on the couch, holding Bella.

The phone rang.

"Well, hey stranger. I haven't seen much of you in months. I'm missing my best friend." Sheila's voice was chipper and alive.

Vanessa felt a surge of positive energy at hearing her friend's voice.

"Hey, I've missed you too. I don't ever see you at work and I pretty much get home and fall into bed.

"Oh, I thought you were better since you went back to work."

"I am, I really am. I'm just still tired after I work, that's all. Doctors say I'm in remission. My treatments are finished. It's just a matter of me finishing my healing process." Vanessa smiled to herself. "I'm supposed to be hurrying that process along by eating properly no less than three times a day." She chuckled. "I'm lucky if I get one meal down. I've just lost interest in food."

Sheila sighed. "Well, I'm going to help fix that, at least for today. You're coming to lunch with me. Or, I'm bringing it to you. Whichever, we're doing it."

Vanessa's smile brightened. Sheila was so thoughtful. "Here's fine. Lamar's working so he won't be in our hair."

Sheila laughed. "Too bad. I won't be able to give him the evil eye. I'm on my way."

Sheila walked in the door with food, a bottle of wine, and a big smile on her face.

"How'd you know I was out of wine?" Vanessa hugged her friend warmly.

"Oh, I don't know, I just figured you might be ready for a little indulgence." Sheila held her thumb and index finger an inch apart.

Vanessa chuckled. "Come on. Let's get our back—together lunch going. I'm still on ginger ale, by the way, but I would have felt awful not being able to offer you any.

After lunch—Vanessa did pretty well, eating half of hers—they went to the rose garden.

Vanessa told her friend of the ups and downs she'd had with Lamar. She didn't mention the closed-fist incident. She was embarrassed by it; her still being with him and a threat of danger in the air.

She did mention the outburst, and showed Sheila the texts and pictures Lamar and Millie had shared.

"You know, all this talk has got me yearning for a glass of that wine. I think I'll have some," Vanessa confessed.

"I got it." Sheila got up and brought a glass. "I can't believe you haven't had this yearning before with everything going on."

"Oh, I've had the yearning, all right. Lamar drinks me out of house and home. If I bring a bottle of wine home, it's gone the next day. Beer, liquor, wine, he drinks it all; and drinks, and drinks. He's out of a job half the time, so guess who ends up paying." Vanessa shook her head.

"Say, I know he's working now, but do you think he'd be free to do some work on my house? I need our back patio repoured or something. At least I think that's what Steven said we needed. The boys have ruined it." Sheila rolled her eyes.

"I'll ask him. I think he said this job's about finished up. That'd be great. Get some money coming in instead of facing another drought and piled up bills.

*   *   *

Vanessa had three days off. Her boss at the hospital was very considerate of her condition and Vanessa told her many times how much she appreciated the consideration. Her boss would say, "Hey, you're one of my best technicians. You're great with patients and the most reliable person I've got."

Vanessa was in bed taking a nap when the phone rang.

"Hello," she said sleepily.

"Vanessa? This is Jake. Jake Hightower? We met a few years back when Lamar brought you to meet me?"

"Oh, yes, I remember. How are you, Jake? I recall you have such a lovely home."

"Well, thank you. Umm, listen Vanessa, this is going to seem a little awkward, but I felt compelled to make this call."

Vanessa was confused. She'd met Jake just the once. He seemed to be a very nice man, but why was he calling her? "Okay, I guess. Go on, Jake."

"Well, you struck me as a very nice lady, and a good person."

"Thank you, Jake, but I don't understand."

"I just don't want you to get taken advantage of."

A knot cramped Vanessa's stomach. She got up from her bed and went into the living room where she could be near Bella.

"You see, I've known Lamar for over thirty years. He was down on his luck, out of a job, and he came to me with an idea. He'd rent my stables to his friends, then charge them for the space. He'd keep his cut for taking care of them, then give me the rest for rent." He paused.

Vanessa knew in her heart what was coming next.

"Well, I thought it was a great idea. I had a contractual agreement drawn up and we both signed it." Jake cleared his throat.

"The first couple of months went great. Then for the better part of a year, I didn't receive anything for the rent.

"Look, the reason I'm telling you this is that I can't stand by and let a nice lady like you be taken advantage of; made a fool of. With someone of your caliber, I'm sure it would be humiliating."

"I'm not sure I follow you, Jake." Vanessa's heart clenched.

"Well, you see, all that time, Lamar had been collecting from his friends, but he was keeping all the money. Then the friends eventually went to other stables because Lamar wasn't cleaning them or keeping up with the supplies for the horses.

"He's a con artist, Vanessa."

The largest dragonfly discovered in the world had a wingspan of over 2 feet and lived in the early Permian period some 280 million years ago.

30

After she thanked Jake for his kindness in caring about her and hung up, Vanessa burst out crying.

Her heart told her she should heed his warning. Her heart told her she loved Lamar, no matter his faults. Everyone had faults, *she* had faults.

She knew Lamar was capable of doing just what Jake had said. But Jake was an acquaintance, *she* was his woman.

Lamar had his ugly moments, but there were times when he was so loving, so caring. No one could fake that, he loved her.

After stewing over the phone call, she composed herself and called her best friend.

"I just had an interesting phone call." Vanessa proceeded to tell Sheila what Jake had said.

"I'm so confused, Sheila. I know he loves me. After the Millie thing, I can't believe he'd do anything to break my heart. I'm pretty sure he lied, but I think it was because he didn't want to hurt me."

"I'm pretty sure he lied, too. You know he got caught having an affair with a church member when he was married," Sheila retorted.

"He told me about that—"

Sheila interrupted her. "It's amazing to me how somebody could turn out like that coming from such a good family." She prattled on. "You know, he used to live next door to Mr. Hill, and Mr. Hill said he came in and out at all hours of the night." Sheila clicked her tongue. "He's a real womanizer, that one. I told you all this before. I'd pay attention to what Jake told you. I warned you about him, Nessa."

Vanessa rose to Lamar's defense. She was tired of everyone trashing her man. "Well, he loves me. He's my companion and my lover. Not everybody's relationship is perfect. Look at yours. Sometimes I don't think you even *like* Steven," she said firmly.

"You're right. Sometimes I don't, but it's security, baby. Besides, I usually get to do what I want." Sheila sighed.

"Look, I don't mean to dump all over your man. I know you love him. We'll forget it. You need to follow your heart. Just be mindful, huh?"

Vanessa consented. "I will. Thanks for lending an ear. I guess my mind was already made up before I called you."

*　　*　　*

Lamar had been working on Sheila's project for a few weeks when he started leaving the house later and coming home after dinner was over.

Vanessa observed this for a few days, then one morning she decided to address it in a roundabout way.

"Do you want me to make a casserole for dinner? That way you can just put it in the oven to heat it up when you get home."

Lamar turned sharply to her. "Is that some kind of comment? Who gives a shit when I get home? It's really none of your business." He slammed his hands down on the table. The coffee cups rattled. "I'm workin' right? I'm bringin' your precious damn money home, ain't I?"

His eyes bulged dangerously. So dangerously, Vanessa felt threatened enough to change her demeanor.

Submissively she said, "I was just worried you might need something besides leftovers or take out. I wanted you to enjoy a good meal. You've been working so hard." Her heart raced.

He studied her face for a full minute, looking for telltale signs of deception. Then his shoulders relaxed. "Thanks, but don't worry about it. I'm good." He drained his coffee. "It's all good."

He went out of the house, slamming the door.

Having the day off, Vanessa sat back down at the table and sipped her coffee. She'd lost her appetite for breakfast. Knowing she needed to build her strength back—she'd not fully recovered her health—she made a piece of toast and nibbled on it.

Thoughts of Jake's phone call, and Sheila's comments ran through her mind. She'd seen no tenderness from Lamar for close to a month.

'A womanizer, that one. Used to live next door to Mr. Hill.' *Asking around gives her that information? How does she know these things? What does she know about his family? Why would she know about his family?*

The doorbell rang.

"Hey stranger, it's just me." Sheila called from the living room. "The door wasn't locked, so I let myself in." She sauntered into the kitchen.

Vanessa didn't know whether to feel invaded and angry, or glad to see her friend.

Sheila's mouth dropped open when she saw Vanessa's face. "Oh my, God. What's wrong? Are you okay?" She knelt beside her friend's chair and enclosed her with tender arms.

Emotions from one gambit to another had gone through Vanessa in the past four hours. At the moment, in her friend's embrace, she felt grateful.

"I've gone from suspicious, to fear, to grief, to anger, and back again this morning. I just don't know how much I can take." Vanessa broke down in tears.

Sheila held her tight until her sobs subsided.

Sheila kissed her forehead. "Now, lets get you dressed. There's no way you can pull yourself together in a bathrobe at 2:00 p.m. in the afternoon." She helped Vanessa out of her chair and guided her to her bedroom.

"You wash your face and get your clothes on. I'm making lunch and pouring us a glass of wine."

Vanessa opened her mouth to protest.

Sheila waggled a finger at her. "Nope, no ifs, ands, or buts. We're having lunch and wine." She softly closed the door.

After a lunch of mushroom omelet—something Sheila felt Vanessa could keep down with her nerves so frayed—they sat in the rose garden.

"How did you know I needed you?" Vanessa asked.

Sheila's jaw dropped, but quickly recovered. She smiled.

"Ever hear of woman's intuition? Well it's even stronger with best friends." Sheila winked.

Vanessa had told Sheila about the later hours for Lamar, and the events of that morning. Then she sat in silence for a few moments thinking.

"Say, I was wondering. How do you know all that stuff you told me about Lamar?"

Sheila looked at her with wide eyes. "Well, I told you, I asked around. I asked around a lot, of course. You don't think I wouldn't find out as much as I could about somebody that's in your home and in your heart?" Sheila pointed to her. "You're my girl!"

Blue-eyed darner females employ a variety of tricks to avoid mating. When it comes to avoiding sexually aggressive males, some female dragonflies play dead.

31

*L*amar came in the door whistling. He was earlier than he had been in days. Vanessa had been napping in the bedroom, but woke from her doze when she heard him come in.

His arms circled around her. He nuzzled her neck and said, "I'm sorry, baby. I've been worried about my mom, but there's no reason I should take it out on you." He began unbuttoning her blouse. "You're the most beautiful woman I've ever known. How about we make that casserole together . . . after we take care of what I'm *really* hungry for."

After dark they both went in the kitchen, put together snacks, and sat down with wine; the casserole forgotten.

The tenderness and love making lasted a few weeks. Vanessa began to relax back into the routine of having a good relationship.

Lamar's money became sporadic. She asked him about it as gently as possible when she received a past due notice from the electric company.

"Oh, I thought this bill was paid. My check doesn't come in until Friday."

He took the bill from her and looked at it. "Oh, I took care of it. They must have sent this out right before." He threw it in the trash. "Don't worry about it."

"Okay, are you finished with Sheila's project?"

He was silent for a moment, then looked at her. "Nah, not yet. I'm waitin' on her. She said she had to accumulate more money before I could finish. I'm waitin' on her to call."

Vanessa figured he must be on another job since he went to work every day. She was afraid of disturbing the calm waters by asking, so she let it go.

A week and a half later, Vanessa came home from work, walked into the house and flicked the light switch.

Nothing happened.

She went to the kitchen, got a flash light and went

to the breaker box. She switched the breaker off, then on again.

Nothing.

Why would he lie to me about that?

Vanessa dialed the electric company and told them her power was cut off. They assured her the bill had not been paid. They'd sent out two warnings of a cut off date. She paid it over the phone, but the power would not be on until the next day.

She got a yogurt out of the fridge, sat on the couch, and waited for Lamar to get home. Bored after an hour she decided to call Sheila.

"Hey what's up?" Sheila asked.

"Not me, I can tell you that," Vanessa replied.

"What's wrong? Is it him again? That bastard," Sheila spat.

"Oh, I don't know if it was a mix up or if he out and out lied to me. But I have no power. The bill wasn't paid." She hated that she was defensive when Sheila attacked him; which happened all the time.

"I don't know what to think anymore, Sheila. I'm on a rollercoaster from hell," Vanessa lamented.

Tired, Vanessa signed off and went to bed.

She woke up to a dark empty house the next morning. Deciding to grab breakfast on the way, she dressed and went to work.

That evening, Lamar came in all apologies. "Oh, baby. I realized I hadn't paid the power bill after all. I went by there to get it handled and they said it was paid yesterday. I'm sorry. I got stuck with mom last night. Are you okay?"

How did he know the power was off?

She just nodded. Too confused and tired to argue.

Two weeks went by. No money from Lamar, though he left for work every day. He was more distant than ever.

He was getting ready to leave for work; it was Vanessa's day off.

"Have you heard from Sheila yet?" She asked him.

"No, why?" He sneered.

"Well, she at least paid you every two weeks. I was just wondering if we were going to have anything coming in soon." She sipped her coffee, heart in her throat.

He turned; his fists clenched to his side.

"Be honest with me, Lamar. Have you taken up with Millie, or some one else again?" She forced herself to breath.

He pointed his finger at her. "I tol' you I didn't have no affair wit dat girl. When you gonna listen to me, bitch? Trust me . . ." his eyes bulged, "you don't want to go down that road. You just think about dat." He stormed out of the house.

Vanessa released her held breath, shaking.

Later that morning the phone rang. It was Christine, her cousin Michael's wife.

"Hey, I was just calling to check on you. How're you feeling these days. Michael and I wanted to stop by and see you; make sure you're okay, but we've been so busy."

"Oh, hey, Christine. I'm okay. Thanks for checking on me."

"You don't sound okay, Nessa, what's going on?" Christine sounded worried.

"It's just . . . personal stuff, ya know, with Lamar."

"What's going on, honey?"

"It's been a roller coaster, Chrissie. He's not bringing any money in. The only time he's romantic is after an argument. He stays out all night and says he was at his mom's. I don't know. I just don't know what to think." Vanessa's eyes teared up.

"Well, it sounds like something's going on. I saw him the other day, talking to that friend of yours. How well do you know her, anyway?"

"What? You mean Sheila? Not a chance. She'd never do anything to hurt me. That's my *girl.*"

Vanessa thanked Christine for calling and hung up.

That weekend Vanessa walked into the bedroom to find Lamar laying clothes out on the bed. "Hey, where you going?" she asked.

"I told this guy I'd go and check out a job he's got; give him a bid. I'll be back this evening." He got into the shower.

She started tidying up the bedroom. His phone rang. It was laying on the bed. She went over and picked it up to see who was calling.

It was Sheila.

A cold sweat broke out down her back. Then, she shook her head.

"It's probably about her back deck. She's finally calling him back to work," she said under her breath.

Nevertheless, a knot had formed in her stomach. She couldn't shake it for the rest of the day.

*   *   *

Dragonflies are swift hunters, but research shows that they aren't turning and diving in reaction to their prey's movements — they're predicting those movements before they occur.

32

*L*amar came out of the bedroom dressed in his nicest jeans and shirt. He saw Vanessa looking him up and down, poked his chest out, and said, "Good for landin' a job, huh?"

She smiled half-heartedly. "I heard your phone ring, I didn't know if you were out of the shower or not."

"Oh, it was Adam, wanting to see if I needed him on his off days." He gave her his two-fingered salute. "See ya later."

Vanessa sat stunned. *He just lied to me.*

All the reasons for him to do so ran across her mind; He was going to turn Sheila down and didn't want Vanessa to know. He was going to work and didn't want Vanessa asking for the money he'd make. Or something else—something she dare not think about.

* * *

After work the next day, Vanessa walked to her car and saw Sheila coming that way. Everything Christine had said surfaced in her mind.

She raised her hand and waved. *I'll at least get to the bottom of some things.*

"Hey, Sheila. I just got a glimpse of you at work today. How'd it go?"

"Oh, not too bad. How was yours?" Sheila put her purse in the car, turned back around and hugged Vanessa.

They chatted a moment about Steven and the boys.

Then Vanessa said, "Oh. I meant to ask, did Lamar ever get in touch with you? He said you needed to wait a bit while you accumulated more money for the job. He said he was going to contact you and ask how things were."

Sheila's face looked as though she'd been struck. "I was . . . Oh, um . . . I . . . Uh, yes. I think he said . . . that he was free next week. Yes, and that he'd come over then."

Vanessa had watched Sheila stammer over this scenario with growing horror. To hide her blaze of anger, she quickly looked at her watch. "Oh, my goodness. I should be at the grandkids school. Yes, well, that's great. It'll be good for him to get paid again." She turned and trotted to her own car, leaving Sheila with her mouth hanging open.

Vanessa's face was burning hot. She was grateful for the cover of her car.

Something is going on here. I can't believe my best friend in the world would betray me. Maybe she's trying to talk him into treating me better and doesn't want me to know.

That's got to be it. Sheila's my best friend. She's stuck with me through this whole sickness, and Lamar's sporadic behavior like a champ. She's been nothing but supportive.

"What's wrong with me?" Feeling guilty for suspecting her dear friend she drove home near tears. Vowing she would talk to Sheila and tell her everything, she walked in the door of her home.

Lamar was laying on the couch drinking a beer. He didn't even look up at her when she walked in.

"Look," she said, "I know something's wrong, Lamar. I just don't know what it is. Don't you want to be here anymore?"

He jumped up off the couch, making her cringe. "What. You think you can get rid of me that easy?" Spittle flew from his mouth. "I'm sick and tired of being your chauffer, taking you to doctor's visits, shopping for your damn groceries. I break my back being your caretaker, giving you all this money, then when you start to get better, you don't need Lamar no more." He pointed to his chest.

"I suppose you'll go back to Kevin, see if you can mooch off'a him for a while. Maybe he'll buy you another fucking Gauche tote. You never had that look of joy over anything *I* ever did for ya. Yeah, I saw that picture of you and him; the day I moved in. I saw that damn tote too, I looked it up, almost $2,000. What thanks do I get for *everything* I've done all these years." His spittle spattered her face, he was so close. "It may not have been nice things, but I've been caretaking my ass off for you. Talk about me behind my back."

His voice took on a sing song high pitched tone. "Oh, he talks like an illiterate hick; he chews with his mouth open; his ears stick out; he drinks me out of house and home." He guzzled the rest of his beer down. "Is something wrong? You bet your sweet ass something's wrong," He poked her in the chest. "And it's you! What a fuckin' bitch. You best be gone when I come back if you know what's good for you." He slammed the door.

Dumbfounded, Vanessa just stood there, her mouth open, purse on her shoulder, gaping at the closed door.

She started shaking. With each sob, her tremors grew worse. She'd registered his bulging eyes, his clenched fists, the snarl on his face. She knew what they meant. *I need to get out of here.*

Her phone rang. It was Christine again. "Hi, Christine."

Her cousin's wife heard Vanessa's distress and was immediately alarmed.

"Vanessa! What's wrong?"

"We—we just had an argument." Vanessa sobbed.

She told Christine all that was said. She was frightened.

"Vanessa. *You* don't leave your home. That's *your* home. You make *him* leave. I know you're scared, put 911 on the speed dial. I know how these punks are, at heart they are cowards." Christine paused.

"I know you don't want to hear this, but you're tougher than you know. Look at what all you've been through."

"I know, Chrissie. And yes, I am scared. But I've worked hard for this home. I just don't know where he got all that information. I can't think of who I've confided in that would tell him all those things I said."

"Well, you rejected the idea before, maybe it's time to think about it again. How well do you know that Sheila person?"

"Oh, it just can't be Chrissie. Sheila's my girl. She's been with me every step of the way. I even had my medical records turned over to her, you know, she's the one who gets called if something happens. She's the one who makes the decisions if I can't. It just can't be, that's my girl, there."

"All right. I just ask that you think about it. I'm a phone call away, Nessa. You call me if you need me, or Michael, we'll be there." She hung up.

Vanessa *did* think about it. She'd locked herself in her bedroom in case Lamar was still volatile if and when he got home.

Her thoughts raced through her mind: Sheila showing up to the house with her skirt split up to her crotch, Sheila's comment, 'If you don't want to handle that, I will.' She and Sheila in her rose garden, Vanessa telling her, her feelings for Lamar, even though he talked like an illiterate hick, his ears—

Her face reddened with heat. *By God, if it worked once, it'll work again.* "I'm pulling those phone records."

Dragonflies lack humans' big brains, but according to new research these insects have brain cells capable of feats previously seen only in primates.

33

Vanessa's heart became a hard cold stone. It was hard to breathe.

She read on:

* June 2- Can you believe that whiney bitch said, "I was waiting for you to show up for Mr. Smith's funeral." LOL

* Yeah, about the time they were lowering his coffin in the ground, was about the time I was deep inside you.

* Oh, baby, I'll never forget that moment. God bless, good old dead Mr. Smith.

* May 12- Ooh, you got me hot with that outfit.

* That's the first time I saw that package of yours. When we gonna put that to use? Oh, God. I just got damp panties.

Vanessa scrolled down quickly, not able to stomach it all.

*Aug 20- I'm so sick and tired of hauling her around, feeding her.

* I would wish she'd just choke one day; but I'm not in her will yet. I need to fix that.

* I know baby. We just need another couple of nights together. I'll make you forget all about her.

* I gotta work. Bitch is on me for money. Your old man ain't gonna give you more for that deck any time soon.

* You know how to work a short day, don't ya? Bring it over, baby. I'm hungry. Besides, you know she's probably off with some man anyway. She flaunts it all over at work.

Vanessa scrolled down to the end.

* 2 hours ago -Meet me at our spot. I just layed in to the bitch. I gotta see you first, but we gotta lay low for a while, she's startin to suspect something.

* I know.

I can't take the pain of it. It's too much.

Tears ran down her face. She felt like there was nowhere for her to turn.

*   *   *

Lamar came home the next day. "I'm sorry, baby. I don't know why I lose my temper like that." He came closer to her and leaned down to kiss her.

Vanessa jerked her head back. "Just what is it you have to talk to Sheila about? And don't bother lying, I know you've talked to her every day."

He stood abruptly and looked down at her sitting on the couch. A mixture of emotions crossed his face as he met her blazing eyes. Confusion—fear—guilt—anger—back to confusion.

"You," he spat.

She threw the pile of papers she had clutched in her hand at his face. "That's right. And a lot of other things, as well."

He opened his mouth to speak.

She held up her hand, palm out. "Don't even bother. Nothing comes out of your mouth but lies. But you need to start looking for somewhere else to live. I'm through."

She walked into her bedroom, closed, and locked the door. She picked up the phone and dialed Steven's number. She knew Sheila would be at work.

"Steven? This is Vanessa. I thought you ought to know, Lamar and your wife have been having an affair. I thought it only fair that you should know. I just found out myself."

"Oh, now, Vanessa. Don't go starting rumors because you and Lamar are having problems. Sheila told me you guys were on the rocks for some time now." Steven said condescendingly.

"I have proof Steven—I."

He cut her off. "Look Vanessa, I know it's natural to accuse others of having the behavior that we're guilty of ourselves. So don't go dragging our family into—"

She hung up on him.

*   *   *

Vanessa went to the kitchen and got a glass of wine. There was a note on the table.

Vanessa, I know I did wrong. Maybe I just can't help myself. I got no excuse. But I love you. I don't have no where else to go right now. I'll do my best to be good from now on. You deserve that. Please give me another chance. I'll look for another place if you still want me to.

Lamar

Vanessa sat down at the table and sipped her wine. She read the note through twice more, then burst into tears.

Hours later Vanessa's phone rang. She was sitting in her rose garden. "Hello?"

"Hi, Vanessa. This is Alice, Steven's sister?" Her voice was strained.

"Hi, Alice. What's going on?"

"Well, I was over visiting the boys. Steven told Sheila what you'd said. Look, I know what she's like. Anyways, Sheila's on the warpath. She said she was going over there to kick your ass. I just thought you ought to know."

"Thanks, Alice. I appreciate you telling me." They hung up.

She hadn't made up her mind about letting Lamar stay. She certainly wasn't ready to give him another chance.

He walked in the door sheepishly.

"Your girl's coming over to kick my ass." Her comment was met with silence.

He sat on the couch and stared at the floor.

Vanessa got up and went into her bedroom. She locked the door and went to bed.

Sheila never showed.

*   *   *

The next day at work went smoothly. Sheila was off. Vanessa walked into records. John looked at her and did a double take.

"Girl?"

"Don't ask, John. Maybe later." She gathered her charts and went to work.

The next day was Sunday, Vanessa was off work. Exhausted from her emotional turmoil, she slept in. The phone woke her up. It was Alice.

"Vanessa, I guess I shouldn't have involved myself, but I can't just stand back and watch a good person done so dirty. I asked Sheila why she'd do something like that to her best friend. She punched me and knocked me down. Steven just stood there and watched."

After the call, Vanessa realized she was going to have to face this. If there was trouble at work, she didn't want to lose her job.

She called her supervisor. "I'm sorry to bother you at home. I love my job. I love my patients. I don't want any trouble, but I've heard there might be. Here's what's going on." She told her the whole story, texts and all.

Her supervisor listened in silence, then thanked Vanessa for calling her.

We'll see what happens tomorrow, I guess.

A **"wonder animal"** is the spirit animal of the dragonfly. It also represents the purity of being and urges people to take chances. It helps them understand that they can fully realize their potential.

34

*H*er arms full of charts, Vanessa came out of Records. She was heading toward the equipment room looking down, not watching where she was going. Then she saw a pair of shoes, unmoving, standing steadfastly.

She almost bumped into Sheila. The look on Sheila's face was pure hatred.

"What's going on? Why are you starting shit with my family? Huh? Why?" Sheila poked Vanessa in the chest.

"Look. I don't want any trouble." Vanessa was painfully aware that other staff members had stopped and were staring at her.

"Then why'd you start it? Huh?" Sheila took a step toward her.

Vanessa backed up; Sheila kept advancing until she had backed Vanessa all the way to the Records room door.

"You're just a conniving bitch that can't control her man." She poked Vanessa in the chest again.

Out of the corner of her eye, Vanessa saw John pick up the phone.

"Then you go and call my *husband*. Ha! At least I've got one. You know what I'm gonna do to you?" Another poke.

Vanessa lost her balance. Charts spilled out of her arms and clattered to the floor.

Sheila towered over her. "Huh? Do you know what I'm—"

Two security guards grabbed Sheila by the arms. They physically escorted the struggling madwoman out of the building.

Vanessa's supervisor came up. She bent and helped pick up the fallen charts.

She stood and looked a stricken Vanessa in the eyes. Her gaze was kind. "She just lost her job. Don't worry, she won't be back here. I'll have security escort you to your car after work, dear. Are you okay to continue your rounds?"

Vanessa nodded. "Yes, ma'am. Now that that's over, I'll be fine. Thank you."

*   *   *

Vanessa went home to a silent house. Lamar was there, parked on the couch, saying nothing, doing nothing.

She went in the kitchen and made herself dinner. She ate alone at the table, then went out to her rose garden with wine.

Every betrayal crept through her mind. Sheila, her best friend; the lies. She'd been stabbed in the back for years. Her heart felt three times its normal size and nothing but a knot of pain. 'Whiney bitch.' She kept seeing the text over and over.

With tears flowing silently down her cheeks, she took herself to bed and locked the bedroom door.

This became their mute ritual over the next five months. Vanessa eating alone, drinking wine with only the company of her roses, then going to bed behind her locked door.

Lamar's presence was heavy but silent.

One day Vanessa noticed his bags were gone from her closet. She pulled down the ladder to the attic and climbed up. All the boxes he'd stored there were gone. The expensive tote bag and her and Kevin's picture were gone, as well. "It makes no difference." She said to the empty room. "I couldn't stand the sight of it after I kicked Kevin out. He's welcome to it." She sighed heavily. Her heart felt like lead.

She dragged herself through work each day. Her grief was still heavy in her heart, but now that his things were gone, it was accompanied by a stark emptiness.

Michael and Christine came by a few times, bringing take out and a bottle of wine.

"Vanessa, you're losing weight. Why don't you come out with us one evening, meet a few people," Michael suggested.

"Oh, I'm fine here. Thanks, though." She heard the despondency in her own voice and hated it. She forced a smile.

A few days later, she heard a knock at the door. She opened the door to Lamar standing there. His arms were full of grocery bags.

"I thought Bella might like some dog food. I brought you a chicken." His crooked smile surfaced.

Her heart stopped. She felt a rush of anger, a wave of fear, but mostly, her crushing loneliness lifting.

"Okay. I'll make us all something to eat." She stepped back and let him in.

They ate with idle chatter. She recalled how easy it was to be with him.

They ate the leftovers the next evening. He left as he did the evening before. "I've been staying with my mom, lately. I'll see you later."

When she got home from work the next day, she received a text from him.

-You want me to bring another chicken or something else?

-How about something else.

An hour later, he showed up with pizza, and a smile.

Toward the end of the evening Lamar grew more tender. They gravitated to the bedroom.

Vanessa tried to summon the womanly passion she'd felt in the beginning of their relationship. But each touch sent revulsion through her entire body.

She wanted desperately to hold on to a semblance of what they'd had; to ward off her loneliness, but the repulsion was too strong.

In order to hold on what little companionship she could attain from him, she sent her mind away; similar to what a rape victim might do to save their life and their sanity. She lay there, forcing herself not to push him off; just a little longer.

They sat at the table drinking wine. She wanted to shower, to wash off his scent, where he'd touched her, where his mouth had been.

She hated herself for even considering another evening like that. How far could her endurance go? Vanessa screwed up her courage, her crushing loneliness a driving factor, and said, "So . . . are you coming back?"

He finished his wine, stood, and rubbed his bulge against her shoulder. "Baby, I know I blew your mind tonight. I been hungry for you."

He leaned down and licked her neck; his fat tongue leaving a thick wine soured trail of saliva.

Her gut clenched. She was filled with shame at her weakness.

"If I'm welcome, I'll be back to blow your mind over and over again. Like I said, I been hungry for you." He left.

She sat at her table understanding the humility to which she'd subjected herself. She'd made the decision to be with him knowing who he was. He brought nothing to the table; he never really had.

She turned her revulsion inward, to herself, until it became anger.

She made the decision to reject him at the door. Enough is enough. She'd never let him in her home or heart again. She only prayed she could stay true to herself. She needn't have worried.

Vanessa never heard from Lamar again.

Each day she came home from work, hopeful and hating herself for it.

Seven weeks later, Christine came over on Vanessa's day off from work.

"I wanted to show you something. I wanted you to see it before someone else told you." Christine hugged her.

"What is it, Chrissie?" Vanessa's heart tightened in her chest.

Christine brought her laptop out of its case. "Let's go to the kitchen table." She led the way.

Vanessa's head began to hurt as panic took hold. "Will you tell me what's going on?"

Christine opened her laptop and went to Facebook. "There." She turned the computer to where Vanessa could see it.

Her mouth dropped open; tears welled in her eyes. There was a picture of Lamar. He was standing by a woman, his arm around her shoulder. They were wearing brilliant smiles, gazing lovingly into each other's eyes.

The caption read: Congratulations to the happy couple, Mr. and Mrs. Lamar Wilson.

With tears spilling down her cheeks, Vanessa looked up at Christine. "The last I heard from him, he said he was probably coming back. Why couldn't he just have had the decency to tell me?"

*   *   *

It took almost a year for Vanessa to turn herself around. She fought through her depression inch by inch. Just when she'd regained her ability to smile at work, having thoughts of going shopping, or maybe going back to the gym, the darkness would pull out its claws and drag her back down.

Her empty heart hurt from what Sheila had done. Then finally, that hurt turned to anger, then hatred. *My best friend for over twenty years. Why?"*

It finally hit her; it didn't matter; it couldn't matter. She made the decision to spend more time with her grandchildren. They were the shining light in her life. She slowly made it to the surface again, this time deciding to write it all down. She prayed she could lose the hatred from her heart. It was only damaging to her. As hard as it was, day by day, word by word, that's what she did; she wrote it down. She got it out of her heart, onto paper, and in to the world. That gave her heart the room it needed to heal.

Her thoughts turned bright and she wondered what Jim was up to. *Maybe I'll just see if my car needs a tune-up.* She shook her head. *Nah, that's a little too forward for me at this point.*

Vanessa's brightness grew every day. She had lunch with new friends and spent time with her family.

She was sipping wine in her rose garden, smiling at her mother's rose bush. An Amberwing dragonfly landed on her hand. *Oh, you beauty.* It's golden wings fanned gently up and down. Vanessa recalled Mr. Smith's nickname for her. "Yes. Mr. Smith, I am finally that dragonfly you always saw in me."

Vanessa made the decision right then, she was going to call Jim the next day.

The phone rang. She picked it up.

"Hey, pretty lady. I was wondering if you might be up for a dinner out. Nothing fancy, you know. I'm kind of a down to earth guy." Jim's voice was gentle and full of sunshine.

The End

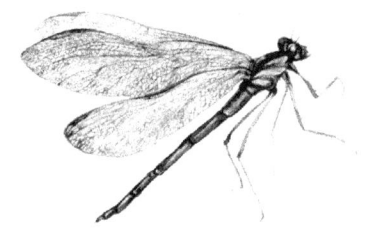

And now,

her life begins

Here are some help lines for women in all circumstances needing assistance or information.

National Hotlines - Victim Connect Resource Center

Domestic Violence Support | The National Domestic Violence Hotline (thehotline.org)

NCW Helpline (ncwwomenhelpline.in)

Free Online Chat therapy

eTherapyPro— Best Overall.
7 Cups— Best for Peer Support.
Free Online Therapy— Best for a Free Assessment.
BlahTherapy— Best for Emotional Support.
TalkwithStranger!— Best for Anonymity.

About the Author

B.J. Flemmings retired from the education system after 35 years of dedicated service.

She enjoyed traveling Europe for a few years, then decided to settle down and put her creativity to work by writing.

Her works are based on real life experiences faced by women of all ethnic backgrounds, young or old, pretty or plain.

Rise Up & Fly will take you through one such woman's struggles caused by innocence and trust. Her growth eventually leads her to triumph.

Ms. Flemmings hails from the mid-west and has a great desire to help women find their courage and self-confidence.

www.ingramcontent.com/pod-product-compliance
Lightning Source LLC
Chambersburg PA
CBHW070851260626
47170CB00007B/2579